THE DEAD BOXER.

By William Carleton

The Dead Boxer

William Carleton

THE WORKS

OF

WILLIAM CARLETON.

VOLUME II.

JANE SINCLAIR.

LHA DHU;
OR, THE DARK DAY.

THE DEAD BOXER.

ELLEN DUNCAN.

THE PROCTOR'S DAUGHTER.

VATENTINE McCLUTCHY,
THE IRISH AGENT

THE TITHE PROCTOR.

THE EMIGRANTS OF AHA-DARRA.

ILLUSTRATED.

NEW YORK:
P. F. COLLIER, PUBLISHER.
1881.

List of Illustrations

Frontispiece

With Stealthy Pace he Crept Over

He Made a Stab at My Neck

The Dead Boxer

CHAPTER I.

One evening in the beginning of the eighteenth century—as nearly as we can conjecture, the year might be that of 1720—some time about the end of April, a young man named *Lamh Laudher* O'Rorke, or Strong-handed O'Eorke, was proceeding from his father's house, with a stout oaken cudgel in his hand, towards an orchard that stood at the skirt of a country town, in a part of the kingdom which, for the present, shall be nameless. Though known by the epithet of *Lamh Laudher*, his Christian name was John; but in those time(s) Irish families of the same name were distinguished from each other by some indicative of their natural position, physical power, complexion, or figure. One, for instance, was called *Parra Ghastha*, or swift Paddy, from his fleetness of foot; another, *Shaun Buie*, or yellow Jack, from his bilious look; a third, *Micaul More*, or big Michael, from his uncommon size; and a fourth, *Sheemus Ruah*, or red James, from the color of his hair. These epithets, to be sure, still occur in Ireland, but far less frequently now than in the times of which we write, when Irish was almost the vernacular language of the country. It was for a reason similar to those just alleged, that John O'Rorke was known as *Lamh Laudher* O'Rorke; he, as well as his forefathers for two or three generations, having been remarkable for prodigious bodily strength and courage. The evening was far advanced as O'Rorke bent his steps to the orchard. The pale, but cloudless sun hung over the western hills, and sun upon the quiet gray fields that kind of tranquil radiance which, in the opening of summer, causes many a silent impulse of delight to steal into the heart. Lamh Laudher felt this; his step was slow, like that of a man who, without being capable of tracing those sources of enjoyment which the spirit absorbs from the beauties of external nature, has yet enough of uneducated taste and feeling within him, to partake of the varied feast which she presents.

As he sauntered thus leisurely along he was met by a woman rather advanced in years, but still unusually stout and muscular, considering her age. She was habited in a red woollen petticoat that reached but a short distance below the knee, leaving visible two stout legs, from which dangled a pair of red garters that bound up her coarse blue hose. Her gown of blue worsted was pinned up, for it did not meet around her person, though it sat closely about her neck. Her grizzly red hair, turned up in front, was bound by a dowd cap without any border, a circumstance which, in addition to a red kerchief, tied over it, and streaming about nine inches down the back, gave to her *tout ensemble* a wild and striking expression. A short oaken staff, hooked under the hand, completed the description of her costume. Even on a first glance there appeared to be something repulsive in her features, which had evidently been much exposed to sun and storm. By a closer inspection one might detect upon their hard angular outline, a character of cruelty and intrepidity. Though her large cheek-bones stood widely asunder, yet her gray piercing eyes were very near each other; her nose was short and sadly disfigured by a scar that ran tranversely across it, and her chin, though pointed, was also deficient in length. Altogether, her whole person had something peculiar and marked about it—so much so, indeed, that it was impossible to meet her without feeling she was a female of no ordinary character and habits.

Lamh Laudher had been, as we have said, advancing slowly along the craggy road which led towards the town, when she issued from an adjoining cabin and approached him. The moment he noticed her he stood still, as if to let her pass and uttered one single exclamation of chagrin and anger.

"*Ma shaughth milia mollach ort, a calliagh!* My seven thousand curses on you for an old hag," said he, and haying thus given vent to his indignation at her appearance, he began to retrace his steps as if unwilling to meet her.

"The son of your father needn't lay the curse upon us so bitterly all out, Lamh Laudher!" she exclaimed, pacing at the same time with vigorous steps until she overtook him.

The young man looked at her maimed features, and as if struck by some sudden recollection, appeared to feel regret for the hasty malediction he had uttered against her. "Nell M'Collum," said he, "the word was rash; and the curse did not come from my heart. But, Nell, who is there that doesn't curse you when they meet you? Isn't it well known that to meet you is another name for falling in wid bad luck? For my part I'd go fifty miles about rather than cross you, if I was bent on any business that my heart 'ud be in, or that I cared any thing about."

"And who brought the bad luck upon me first?" asked the woman. "Wasn't it the husband of the mother that bore you? Wasn't it his hand that disfigured me as you see, when I was widin a week of bein' dacently married? Your father, Lamh Laudher was the man that blasted my name, and made it bitther upon tongue of them that mintions it."

"And that was because he wouldn't see one wid the blood of Lamh Laudher in his veins married to a woman that he had reason to think—I don't like to my it, Nelly—but you know it is said that there was darkness, and guilt, too, about the disappearin' of your child. You never cleared that up, but swore revenge night and day against my father, for only preventin' you from bein' the ruination of his cousin. Many a time, too, since that, has asked you in my own hearing what became of the boy."

The old woman stopped like one who had unexpectedly trod with bare foot upon something sharp enough to pierce the flesh to the bone, and even to grate against it. There was a strong, nay, a fearful force of anguish visible in what she felt. Her brows were wildly depressed from their natural position, her face became pale, her eyes glared upon O'Rorke as if he had planted a poisoned arrow in her breast, she seized him by the arm with a hard pinching grip, and looked for two or three minutes in his face, with an appearance of distraction. O'Rorke, who never feared man, shrunk from her touch, and shuddered under the influence of what had been, scarcely without an exception, called the "bad look." The crone held him tight, however, and there they stood, with their eyes fixed upon each other. From the gaze of intense anguish, the countenance of Nell M'Collum began to change gradually to one of unmingled exultation; her brows were raised to their proper curves, her color returned, the eye corruscated with a rapid and quivering sense of delight, the muscles of the mouth played for a little, as if she strove to suppress a laugh. At length O'Rorke heard a low gurgling sound proceed from her chest; it increased; she pressed his arm more tightly, and in a loud burst of ferocious mirth, which she immediately subdued into a condensed shriek that breathed the very luxury of revenge, she said —

"*Lamh Laudher Oge*, listen — ax the father of you, when you see him, what has become *of his own child* — of the first that ever God sent him; an' listen again — when he tells me what has become of mine, I'll tell him what has become of his, Now go to Ellen — but before you go, let me *cuggher* in your ear that I'll blast you both. I'll make the *Lamh Laudhers, Lamh Lhugs*. I'll make the strong arm the weak arm afore I've done wid 'em."

She struck the point of her stick against the pavement, until the iron ferrule with which it was bound dashed the fire from the stones, after which she passed on, muttering threats and imprecations as she left him.

O'Rorke stood and looked after her with sensations of fear and astonishment. The age was superstitious, and encouraged a belief in the influence of powers distinct from human agency. Every part of Ireland was filled at this time with characters, both male and female, precisely similar to old Nell M'Collum.. The darkness in which this woman walked, according to the opinions of a people but slightly advanced in knowledge and civilization, has been but feebly described to the reader. To meet her, was considered an omen of the most unhappy kind; a circumstance which occasioned the imprecation of Lamh Laudher. She was reported to have maintained an intercourse with the fairies, to be capable of communicating the blight of an evil eye, and to have carried on a traffic which is said to have been rather prevalent in Ireland at the time we speak of — namely, that of kidnapping. The speculations with reference to her object in perpetrating the crimes were strongly calculated to exhibit the degraded state of the people at that period. Some said that she disposed of the children to a certain class of persons in the metropolis, who subsequently sent them to the colonies, when grown, at an enormous profit. Others maintained that she never carried them to Dublin at all, but insisted that, having been herself connected with the fairies, she possessed the power of erasing, by some secret charm, the influence of baptismal protection, and that she consequently acted as agent for the "gentry" to whom she transferred them. Even to this day it is the opinion in Ireland, that the "good people" themselves cannot take away a child, except through the instrumentality of some mortal residing with them, who has been baptized; and it is also believed that no baptism can secure children from them, except that in which the priest has been desired to baptize them with an especial view to their protection against fairy power.

Such was the character which this woman bore; whether unjustly or not, matters little. For the present it is sufficient to say, that after having passed on, leaving Lamh Laudher to proceed in the direction he had originally intended, she bent her steps towards the head inn of the town. Her presence here produced some cautious and timid mirth of which they took care she should not be cognizant. The servants greeted her with an outward show of cordiality, which the unhappy creature easily distinguished from the warm kindness evinced to vagrants whose history had not been connected with evil suspicion and mystery. She accordingly tempered her manner and deportment towards them with consummate skill. Her replies to their inquiries for news were given with an appearance of good humor; but beneath the familiarity of her dialogue there lay an ambiguous meaning and a cutting sarcasm, both of which were tinged with a prophetic spirit, capable, from its equivocal drift, of being applied to each individual whom she addressed. Owing to her unsettled life, and her habit of passing from place to place, she was well acquainted with local history. There lived scarcely a family within a very wide circle about her, of whom she did not know every thing that could possibly be known; a fact of which she judiciously availed herself by allusions in general conversations that were understood only by those whom they concerned. These mysterious hints, oracularly thrown out, gained her the reputation of knowing more than mere human agency could acquire, and of course she was openly conciliated and secretly hated.

Her conversation with the menials of the inn was very short and decisive.

"Sheemus," said she to the person who acted in the capacity of waiter, "where's Meehaul Neil?"

"Troth, Nell, dacent woman," replied the other, "myself can't exactly say that. I'll be bound he's on the *Esker*, looking afther the sheep, poor crathurs, durin' Andy Connor's illness in the small-pock. Poor Andy's very ill, Nell, an' if God hasn't sed it, not expected; glory be to his name!"

"Is Andy ill?" inquired Nell; "and how long?"

"Bedad, going on ten days."

"Well," said the woman, "I knew nothin' about that; but I want to see Meehaul Neil, and I know he's in the house."

"Faix he's not, Nelly, an' you know I wouldn't tell you a lie about it."

"Did you get the linen that was stolen from your masther?" inquired Nell significantly, turning at the same time a piercing glance on the waiter; "an' tell me," she added, "how is Sally Lavery, and where is she?"

"It wasn't got," he replied, in a kind of stammer; "an' as to Sally, the nerra one o' me knows any thing about her, since she left this."

"Sheemus," replied Nell, "you know that Meehaul Neil is in the house; but I'll give you two choices, either to bring me to the speech of him, or else I'll give your masther the name of the thief that stole his linen; ay! the name of the thief that resaved it. I name nobody at present; an' for that matther, I know nothin'. Can't all the world tell you that Nell M'Cullum knows nothin'!"

"*Ghe dhevin*, Nelly," said the waiter, "maybe Meehaul is in the house unknownst to me. I'll try, any how, an' if he's to the fore, it won't be my fault or he'll see you."

Nell, while the waiter went to inform Meehaul, took two ribbons out of her pocket, one white and the other black, both of which she folded into what would appear to a bystander to be a simple kind of knot. When the innkeeper's son and the waiter returned to the hall, the former asked her what the nature of her business with him might be. To this she made no reply, except by uttering the word husht! and pulling the ends, first of the white ribbon, and afterwards of the black. The knot of the first slipped easily from the complication, but that of the black one, after gliding along from its respective ends, became hard and tight in the middle.

"*Tha sha marrho!* life passes and death stays," she exclaimed. "Andy Connor's dead, Meehaul Neil; an' you may tell your father that he must get some one else to look afther his sheep. Ay! he's dead!—But that's past. Meehaul, folly me; it's you I want, an' there's no time to be lost."

She passed out as she spoke, leaving the waiter in a state of wonder at the extent of her knowledge, and of the awful means by which, in his opinion, she must have acquired it.

Meehaul, without uttering a syllable, immediately walked after her. The pace at which she went was rapid and energetic, betokening a degree of agitation and interest on her part, for which he could not account. As she had no object in bringing him far from the house, she availed herself of the first retired spot that presented itself, in order to disclose the purport of her visit. "Meehaul Neil," said she, "we're now upon the Common, where no ear can hear what passes between us. I ax have you spirit to keep your sister Ellen from shame and sorrow?" The young man started, and became strongly excited at such a serious prelude to what she was about to utter.

"*Millia diououl!* woman, why do you talk about shame or disgrace comin' upon any sister of mine?" What villain dare injure her that regards his life? My sisther! Ellen Neil! No, no! the man that 'ud only think of that, I'd give this right hand a dip to the wrist in the best blood of his heart."

"Ay, ay! it's fine spakin': but you don't know the hand you talk of. It's one that you had better avoid than meet. It's the strong hand, an' the dangerous one when vexed. You know Lamh Laudher Oge?"

Meelmul started again, and the crone could perceive by his manner that the nature of the communication she was about to make had been already known to him, though not, she was confident, in so dark and diabolical a shape as that in which she determined to put it.

"Lamh Laudher Oge!" he exclaimed; "surely you don't mane to say that he has any bad design upon Ellen! It's not long since I gave him a caution to drop her, an' to look out for a girl fittin' for his station. Ellen herself knows what he'll get, if we ever catch him spakin' to her again. The day will never come that his faction and ours can be friends."

"You did do that, Meehaul," replied Nell, "an' I know it; but what 'ud you think if he was so cut to the heart by your turnin' round upon his poverty, that he swore an oath to them that I could name, bindin' himself to bring your sister to a state of shame, in order to punish you for your words? That 'ud be great glory over a faction that they hate."

"Tut, woman, he daren't swear such an oath; or, if he swore it fifty times over on his bare knees, he'd ate the stones off o' the pavement afore he'd dare to act upon it. In the first place, I'd prepare him for his coffin, if he did; an' in the next, do you think so inanely of Ellen, as to believe that she would bring disgrace an' sorrow upon herself and her family? No, no, Nell; the old *dioul's* in you, or you're beside yourself, to think of such a story. I've warned her against him, and so did we all; an' I'm sartin' this minute, that she'd not go a single foot to change words with him, unknownst to her friends."

The old woman's face changed from the expression of anxiety and importance that it bore, to one of coarse glee, under which, to those who had penetration sufficient to detect it, lurked a spirit of hardened and reckless ferocity.

"Well, well," she replied, "sure I'm proud to hear what you tell me. How is poor Nanse M'Collum doin' wid yez? for I hadn't time to see her a while agone. I hope she'll never be ashamed or afraid of her aunt, any how. I may say, I'm all that's left to the good of her name, poor girshah."

"What 'ud ail her?" replied Meehaul; "as long a' she's honest an' behaves herself, there's no fear of her. Had you nothing elsa to say to me, Nell?"

The same tumultuous expression of glee and malignity again lit up the features of the old woman, as she looked at him, and replied, with something like contemptuous hesitation, "Why, I don't know that. If you had more sharpness or sinse I might say—Meehaul Neil," she added, elevating her voice, "what do you think I could say, this sacred moment! Your sister! Why she's a good girl!—true enough that: but how long she may be so's another affair. Afeard! Be the ground we stand on, man dear, if you an' all belongin' to you,

The Dead Boxer

had eyes in your heads for every day in the year, you couldn't keep her from young Lamh Laudher. Did you hear anything?"

"I'd not believe a word of it," said Meehaul calmly, and he turned to depart.

"I tell you it's as true as the sun to the dial," replied Nell; "and I tell you more, he's wid her this minnit behind your father's orchard! Ay! an' if you wish you may see them together wid your own eyes, an' sure if you don't b'lieve me, you'll b'lieve them. But, Meehaul, take care of him; for he has his fire-arms; if you meet him don't go empty-handed, and I'd advise you to have the first shot."

"Behind the orchard," said Meehaul, astonished; "where there?"

"Ay, behind the orchard, where they often war afore. Where there? Why, if you want to know that, sittin' on one of the ledges in the Grassy Quarry. That's their sate whenever they meet; an' a snug one it is for them that don't like their neighbors' eyes to be upon them. Go now an' satisfy yourself, but watch them at a distance, an', as you expect to save your sister, don't breathe the name of Nell M'Collum to a livin' mortal."

Meehaul Neil's cheek flushed with deep resentment on hearing this disagreeable intelligence. For upwards of a century before there had subsisted a deadly feud between the Neils and Lamh Laudhers, without either party being able exactly to discover the original fact from which their enmity proceeded. This, however, in Ireland, makes little difference. It is quite sufficient to know that they meet and fight upon every possible opportunity, as hostile factions ought to do, without troubling themselves about the idle nonsense of inquiring why they hate and maltreat each other. For this reason alone, Meehaul Neil was bitterly opposed to the most distant notion of a marriage between his sister and young Lamh Laudher. There were other motives also which weighed, with nearly equal force, in the consideration of this subject. His sister Ellen was by far the most beautiful girl of her station in the whole country,—and many offers, highly advantageous, and far above what she otherwise could have expected, had been made to her. On the other hand, Lamh Laudher Oge was poor, and by no means qualified in point of worldly circumstances to propose for her, even were hereditary enmity out of the question. All things considered, the brother and friends of Ellen would rather have seen her laid in her grave, than allied to a comparatively poor young man, and their bitterest enemy.

Meehaul had but little doubt as to the truth of what Nell M'Collum told him. There was a saucy and malignant confidence in her manner, which, although it impressed him with a sense of her earnestness, left, nevertheless, an indefinite feeling of dislike against her on his mind. He knew that her motive for disclosure was not one of kindness or regard for him or for his family. Nell M'Collum had often declared that "the wide earth did not carry a bein' she liked or loved, but one—not even excepting herself, that she hated most of all." This however was not necessary to prove that she acted rather from the gratification of some secret malice, than from the principle of benevolence. The venomous leer of her eye, therefore, and an accurate knowledge of her character, induced him to connect some apprehension of approaching evil with the unpleasant information she had just given him.

"Well," said Meehaul, "if what you say is true, I'll make it a black business to Lamh Laudher. I'll go directly and keep my eye on them; an' I'll have my fire-arms, Nell; an' by the life that's in me, he'll taste them if he provokes me; an Ellen knows that." Having thus spoken he left her.

The old woman stood and looked after him with a fiendish complacency.

"A black business, will you?" she exclaimed, repeating his words in a soliloquy;—"do so—an' may all that's black assist you in it! Dher Chiernah, I'll do it or lose a fall—I'll make the Lamh Laudhers the Lamh Lhugs afore I've done wid 'em. I've put a thorn in their side this many a year, that'll never come out; I'll now put one in their marrow, an' let them see how they'll bear that. I've left *one* empty chair at their hearth, an' it 'll go hard wid me but I'll lave another."

Having thus expressed her hatred against a family to whom she attributed the calamities that had separated her from society, and marked her as a being to be avoided and detested, she also departed from the Common, striking her stick with peculiar bitterness into the ground as she went along.

CHAPTER II.

In the mean time young Lamh Laudher felt little suspicion that the stolen interview between him and Ellen Neil was known. The incident, however, which occurred to him on his way to keep the assignation, produced in his mind a vague apprehension which he could not shake off. To meet a red-haired woman, when going on any business of importance, was considered at all times a bad omen, as it is in the country parts of Ireland unto this day; but to meet a female familiar with forbidden powers, as Nell M'Collum was supposed to be, never failed to produce fear and misgiving in those who met her. Mere physical courage was no bar against the influence of such superstitions; many a man was a slave to them who never knew fear of a human or tangible enemy. They constituted an important part of the popular belief! for the history of ghosts and fairies, and omens, was, in general, the only kind of lore in which the people were educated; thanks to the sapient traditions of their forefathers.

When Nell passed away from Lamh Laudher, who would fain have flattered himself that by turning back on the way, until she passed him, he had avoided meeting her, he once more sought the place of appointment, at the same slow pace as before. On arriving behind the orchard, he found, as the progress of the evening told him, that he had anticipated the hour at which it had been agreed to meet. He accordingly descended the Grassy Quarry, and sat on a mossy ledge of rock, over which the brow of a little precipice jutted in such a manner as to render those who sat beneath, visible only from a particular point. Here he had scarcely seated himself when the tread of a foot was heard, and in a few minutes Nanse M'Collum stood beside him.

"Why, thin, bad cess to you, Lamh Laudher," she exclaimed, "but it's a purty chase I had afther you."

"Afther me, Nanse? and what's the commission, *cush gastha* (lightfoot)?"

"The sorra any thing, at all, at all, only to see if you war here. Miss Ellen sent me to tell you that she's afeard she can't come this evenin', unknownst to them."

"An' am I not to wait, Nanse?"

"Why, she says she—*will* come, for all that, if she can; but she bid me take your stick from you, for a rason she has, that she'll tell yourself when she sees you."

"Take my stick! Why Nanse, *ma colleen baun*, what can she want with my stick? Is the darlin' girl goin' to bate any body?"

"Bad cess to the know *I* know, Lamh Laudher, barrin' it be to lay on yourself for stalin' her heart from her. Why thin, the month's mether o' honey to you, soon an' sudden, how did you come round her at all?"

"No matter about that, Nanse; but the family's bitther against me?—eh?"

"Oh, thin, in trogs, it's ill their common to hate you as they do; but thin, you see, this faction-work will keep yees asundher for ever. Now gi' me your stick, an' wait, any way, till you see whether she comes or not."

"Is it by Ellen's ordhers you take it, Nanse?"

"To be sure—who else's? but the divil a one o' me knows what she means by it, any how—only that I daren't go back widout it."

"Take it, Nanse; she knows I wouldn't refuse her my heart's blood, let alone a bit of a kippeen."

"A bit of a kippeen! Faix, this is a quare kippeen! Why, it would fell a bullock."

"When you see her, Nanse, tell her to make haste, an' for God's sake not to disappoint me. I can't rest well the day I don't meet her."

"Maybe other people's as bad, for that matter; so good night, an' the mether o' honey to you, soon an' sudden! Faix, if any body stand in my way now, they'll feel the weight of this, any how."

After uttering the last words, she brandished the cudgel and disappeared.

Lamh Laudher felt considerably puzzled to know what object Ellen could have had in sending the servant maid for his staff. Of one thing, however, he was certain, that her motive must have had regard to his own safety; but how, or in what manner, he could not conjecture. It is certainly true some misgivings shot lightly across his imagination, on reflecting that he had parted with the very weapon which he usually brought with him to repel the violence of Ellen's friends, should he be detected in an interview with her. He remembered, too, that he had met unlucky Nell M'Collum, and that the person who deprived him of his principal means of defence was her niece. He had little time, however, to think upon the subject, for in a few minutes after Nanse's departure, he recognized the light quick step of her whom he expected.

The figure of Ellen Neil was tall, and her motions full of untaught elegance and natural grace. Her countenance was a fine oval; her features, though not strictly symmetrical, were replete with animation, and her eyes sparkled with a brilliancy indicative of a warm heart and a quick apprehension. Flaxen hair, long and luxuriant, decided, even at a distant glance, the loveliness of her skin, than which the unsunned snow could not be whiter. If you add to this a delightful temper, buoyant spirits, and extreme candor, her character, in its strongest points, is before you.

On reaching the bottom of the Grassy Quarry, as it was called, she peered under the little beetling cliff that overhung the well-known ledge on which Lamh Laudher sat.

"I declare, John," said she, on seeing him, "I thought at first you weren't here."

"Did you ever know me to be late!—" said John, taking her by the hand, and placing her beside him; "and what would you a' done, Ellen, if I hadn't been here?"

"Why, run home as if the life was lavin' me, for fear of seein' something."

"You needn't be afeard, Ellen, dear; nothing could harm you, at all events. However, puttin' that aside, have you any betther tidin's than you had when we met last?"

"I wish to heaven I had, John! but indeed I have far worse; ay, a thousand times worse. They have all joined against me, an' I'm not to see or speak to you at all."

"That's hard," replied Lamh Laudher, drawing his breath tightly; "but I know where it comes from. I think your father might be softened a little, ay, a great deal, if it wasn't for your brother Meehaul."

"Indeed, Lamh Laudher, you're wrong in that; my father's as bitther against you as he is. It was only on Tuesday evenin' last that they told me, one an' all they would rather see me a corpse than your wife. Indeed an' deed, John, I doubt it never can be."

"There," replied John, "I see plain enough that they'll gain you over at last. That will be the end of it: but if you choose to break the vows and promises that passed between us, you may do so."

"Oh! Lamh Laudher," said Ellen, affected at the imputation contained in his last observation; "don't you treat me with such suspicion. I suffer enough for your sake, as it is. For nearly two years, a day has hardly passed that my family hasn't wrung the burnin' tears from my eyes on your account. Haven't I refused matches that any young woman in my station of life ought to be I proud to accept?"

"You did, Ellen, you did; but still I know how hard it is for you to hould out against the persecution you suffer at home. No, no, Ellen dear, I never doubted you for one minute. All I wondher at is, that such a girl as you ever could think of one so humble as I am, compared to what you'd have a right to expect an' could get."

"Well, but if I'm willin' to prefer you, John?" said Ellen, with a smile.

"One thing I know, Ellen," he replied, "an' that is, that I'm far from bein' worthy of you; an' I ought, if I had a high enough spirit, to try to turn you against me, if it was only that you might marry a man that 'ud have it in his power to make you happier than ever I'll be able to do; any way, than ever it's likely I'll be able to do."

"I don't think, John, that ever money or the wealth of the world made a man an' wife love one another yet, if they didn't do it before; but it has often put their hearts against one another."

The Dead Boxer

"I agree wid you in that, Ellen; but you don't know how my heart sinks when I think of your an' my own poverty. My poor father, since the strange disappearance of little Alice, never was able to raise his head; and indeed my mother was worse. If the child had died, an' that we knew she slept with ourselves, it would be a comfort. But not to know what became of her—whether she was drowned or kidnapped—that was what crushed their hearts. I must say that since I grew up, we're improvin'; an' I hope, God willin', now that my father laves the management of the farm to myself, we'll still improve more an' more. I hope it for their sakes, but—more, if possible, for yours. I don't know what I wouldn't do to make you happy, Ellen. If my life could do it, I think I could lay it down to show the love I bear you. I could take to the highway and rob for your sake, if I thought it would bring me means to make you happy."

Ellen was touched by his sincerity, as well as by the tone of manly sorrow with which he spoke. His last words, however, startled her, when she considered the vehement manner in which he uttered them.

"John," said she, alarmed, "never, while you have life, let me hear a word of that kind out of your lips. No—never, for the sake of heaven above us, breathe it, or think of it. But, I'll tell you something, an' you must hear it, an' bear it too, with patience."

"What is it, Ellen! If it's fair an' manly, I'll be guided by your advice."

"Meehaul has threatened to—to—I mane to say, that you musn't have any quarrel with him, if he meets you or provokes you. Will you promise this?"

"Meenaul has threatened to strike me, has he? An' I, a Lamh Laudher, am to take a blow from a Neil, an' to thank him, I suppose, for givin' it."

Ellen rose up and stood before him.

"Lamh Laudher," said she, "I must now try your love for me in earnest. A lie I cannot tell no more than I can cover the truth. My brother has threatened to strike you, an' as I said afore, you must bear it for his sister's sake."

The Dead Boxer

"No, *dher Chiernah*, never. That, Ellen, is goin' beyant what I'm able to bear. Ask me to cut off my right hand for your sake, an' I'll do it; ask my life, an' I'll give it: but to ask a Lamh Laudher to bear a blow from a Neil—never. What! how could I rise my face afther such a disgrace? How could I keep the country wid a Neil's blow, like the stamp of a thief upon my forehead, an' me the first of my own faction, as your brother is of his. No—never!"

"An' you say you love me, John?"

"Betther than ever man loved woman."

"No, man—you don't," she replied; "if you did, you'd give up something for me. You'd bear that for my sake, an' not think it much. I'm beginin' to believe, Lamh Laudher, that if I was a poor portionless girl, it wouldn't be hard to put me out of your thoughts. If it was only for my own sake you loved me, you'd not refuse me the first request I ever made to you; when you know, too, that if I didn't think more of you than I ought, I'd never make it."

"Ellen, would you disgrace me? Would you wish me to bear the name of a coward? Would you want my father to turn me out of the house? Would you want my own faction to put their feet upon me, an' drive me from among them?"

"John," she replied, bursting into tears, "I do know that it's a sore obligation to lay upon you, when everything's taken into account; but if you wouldn't do this for me, who would you do it for? Before heaven, John, I dread a meetin' between you an' my brother, afther what he tould me; an' the only way of preventin' danger is for you not to strike him. Oh, little you know what I have suffered these two days for both your sakes! Lamh Laudher Oge, I doubt it would be well for me if I had never seen your face."

"Anything undher heaven but what you want me to do, Ellen."

"Oh! don't refuse me this, John. I ask it, as I said, for both your sake, an' for my own sake. Meehaul wouldn't strike an unresistin' man. I won't lave you till you promise; an' if that won't do, I'll go down on my. knees an' ask you for the sake of heaven above, to be guided by me in this."

"Ellen, I'll lave the country to avoid him, if that'll plase you."

16

"No—no—no, John: that doesn't plase me. Is it to lave your father an' family, an' you the staff of their support? Oh, John, give me your promise. Here on my two knees I ask it from you, for my own, for your own, and for the sake of God above us! I know Meehaul. If he got a blow from you on my account, he'd never forgive it to either you or me."

She joined her hands in supplication to him as she knelt, and the tears chased each other like rain down her cheeks. The solemnity with which she insisted on gaining her point staggered Lamh Laudher not a little.

"There must be something undher this," he replied, "that makes you set your heart on it so much. Ellen, tell me the truth; what is it?"

"If I loved you less, John, an' my brother too, I wouldn't care so much about it. Remember that I'm a woman, an' on my knees before you. A blow from you would make him take your life or mine, sooner than that I should become your wife. You ought to know his temper."

"You know, Ellen, I can't at heart refuse you any thing. I will not strike your brother."

"You promise, before God, that no provocation will make you strike him."

"That's hard, Ellen; but—well, I do; before God, I won't—an' it's for your sake I say it. Now, get up, dear, get up. You have got me to do what no mortal livin' could bring me to but yourself. I suppose that's what made you send Nanse M'Collum for my staff?"

"Nancy M'Collum! When?"

"Why, a while ago. She tould me a quare enough story, or rather no story at all, only that you couldn't come, an' you could come, an' I was to give up my staff to her by your ordhers."

"She tould you false, John. I know nothing about what you say."

"Well, Ellen," replied Lamh Laudher, with a firm seriousness of manner, "you have brought me into danger. I doubt, without knowin' it. For my own part, I don't care so much. Her unlucky aunt met me comin' here this evenin', and threatened both our family and yours. I know she would sink us into the earth if she could. Either she or your brother is at the bottom of this business, whatever it is. Your brother I don't fear; but she is to be dreaded, if, all's true that's said about her."

"No, John—she surely couldn't have the heart to harm, you an' me. Oh, but I'm light now, since you did what I wanted you. No harm can come between you and Meehaul; for I often heard him say, when speakin' about his faction fights, that no one but a coward would, strike an unresistin' man. Now come and see me pass the Pedlar's Cairn, an' remember that you'll thank me for what I made you do this night. Come quickly—I'll be missed."

They then passed on by a circuitous and retired path that led round the orchard, until he had conducted her in safety beyond the Pedlar's Cairn, which was so called from a heap of stones that had been loosely piled together, to mark the spot as the scene of a murder, whose history, thus perpetuated by the custom of every passenger casting a stone upon the place, constituted one of the local traditions of the neighborhood.

After a tender good-night, given in a truly poetical manner under the breaking light of a May moon, he found it necessary to retrace his steps by a path which wound round the orchard, and terminated in the public entrance to the town. Along this suburban street he had advanced but a short way, when he found himself overtaken and arrested by his bitter and determined foe, Meehaul Neil. The connection betwixt the promise that Ellen had extorted from him and this rencounter with her brother flashed upon him forcibly: he resolved, however, to be guided by her wishes, and with this purpose on his part, the following dialogue took place between the heads of the rival factions. When we say, however, that Lamh Laudher was the head of his party, we beg to be understood as alluding only to his personal courage and prowess; for there were in it men of far greater wealth and of higher respectability, so far as mere wealth could confer the latter.

"Lamh Laudher," said Meehaul, "whenever a Neil spakes to you, you may know it's hot in friendship."

"I know that, Meehaul Neil, without hearin' it from you. Spake, what have you to say?"

"There was a time," observed the other, "when you and I were enemies only because our cleaveens were enemies but now there is, an' you know it, a blacker hatred between us."

"I would rather there was not, Meehaul; for my own part, I have no ill-will against either you or yours, all you know that; so when you talk of hatred, spake only for yourself."

"Don't be mane, man," said Neil; "don't make them that hates you despise you into the bargain."

Lamh Laudher turned towards him fiercely, and his eye gleamed with passion; but he immediately recollected himself, and simply said—

"What is your business with me this night, Meehaul Neil?"

"You'll know that soon enough—sooner, maybe, than you wish. I now ask you to tell me, if you are an honest man, where you have been?"

"I am as honest, Meehaul, as any man that ever carried the name of Neil upon him, an' yet I won't tell you that, till you show me what right you have to ask me."

"I b'lieve you forget that I'm Ellen Neil's brother: now, Lamh Laudher, as her brother, I choose to insist on your answering me."

"Is it by her wish?"

"Suppose I say it is."

"Ay! but I won't suppose that, till you lay your right hand on your heart, and declare as an honest man, that—tut, man—this is nonsense. Meehaul, go home—I would rather there was friendship between us."

"You were with Ellen, this night in the! Grassy Quarry."

"Are you sure of that?"

"I saw you both—I watched you both; you left her beyond the Pedlar's Cairn, an' you're now on your way home."

"An' the more mane you, Meehaul, to become a spy upon a girl that you know is as pure as the light from heaven. You ought to blush for doubtin' sich a sister, or thinkin' it your duty to watch her as you do."

"Lamh Laudher, you say that you'd rather there was no ill-will between us."

"I say that, God knows, from my heart out."

"Then there's one way that it may be so. Give up Ellen; you'll find it for your own interest to do so."

"Show me that, Meehaul."

"Give her up, I say, an' then I may tell you."

"Meehaul, good-night. Go home."

They had now entered the principal street of the town, and as they proceeded in what appeared to be an earnest, perhaps a friendly conversation, many of their respective acquaintances, who lounged in the moonlight about their doors, were not a little surprised at seeing them in close conference. When Lamh Laudher wished him good night, he had reached an off street which led towards his father's house, a circumstance at which he rejoiced, as it would have been the means, he hoped, of terminating a dialogue that was irksome to both parties. He found himself, however, rather unexpectedly and rudely arrested by his companion.

"We can't part, Lamh Laudher," said Meehaul seizing him by the collar, "'till this business is settled—I mane till you promise to give my sister up."

"Then we must stand here, Meehaul, as long as we live—an' I surely won't do that."

"You must give her up, man."

"Must! Is it must from a Neil to a Lamh Laudher? You forgot yourself, Meehaul: you are rich now, an' I'm poor now; but any old friend can tell you the differ between your grandfather an' mine. Must, indeed!"

"Ay; must is the word, I say; an' I tell you that from this spot you won't go till you swear it, or this stick—an' it's a good one—will bring you to submission."

"I have no stick, an' I suppose I may thank you for that."

"What do you mane?" said Neil; "but no matter—I don't want it. There—to the divil with it;" and as he spoke he threw it over the roof of the adjoining house.

"Now give up my sister or take the consequence."

"Meehaul, go home, I say. You know I don't fear any single man that ever breathed; but, above all men on this earth, I wish to avoid a quarrel with you. Do you think, in the mean time, that even if I didn't care a straw for your sister, I could be mane enough to let myself be bullied out of her by you, or any of your faction? Never, Meehaul; so spare your breath, an' go home."

Several common acquaintances had collected about them, who certainly listened to this angry dialogue between the two faction leaders with great interest. Both were powerful men, young, strong, and muscular. Meehaul, of the two, was taller, his height being above six feet, his strength, courage, and activity, unquestionably very great. Lamh Laudher, however, was as fine a model of physical strength, just proportion, and manly beauty as ever was created; his arms, in particular, were of terrific strength, a physical advantage so peculiar to his family as to occasion the epithet by which it was known. He had scarcely uttered the reply we have I written, when Meehaul, with his whole! strength, aimed a blow at his stomach, which the other so far turned aside, as to bring it I higher up on his chest. He staggered back, after receiving it, about seven or eight yards, but did not fall. His eye literally blazed, and for a moment he seemed disposed to act! under the strong impulse of self-defence. The solemnity of his promise to Ellen, however, recurred to him in time to restrain his uplifted arm. By a strong and sudden effort he endeavored to compose himself, and succeeded. He approached Meehaul, and with as much calmness as he could assume, said—

"Meehaul, I stand before you an' you may strike, but I won't return your blows: I have reasons for it, but I tell you the truth."

"You won't fight?" said Meehaul, with mingled rage and scorn.

"No," replied the other, "I won't fight you."

A murmur of "shame" and "coward" was heard from those who had been drawn together by their quarrel.

"*Dher ma chorp*," they exclaimed with astonishment, "but Lamh Laudher's afeard of him!—the *garran bane's* in him, now that he finds he has met his match."

"Why, hard fortune to you, Lamh Laudher, will you take a blow from a Neil? Are you goin' to disgrace your name?"

"I won't fight him," replied he to whom they spoke, and the uncertainty of his manner was taken for want of courage.

"Then," said Meehaul, "here, before witnesses, I give you the coward, that you may carry the name to the last hour of your life."

He inflicted, when uttering the words, a blow with his open hand on Lamh Laudher's cheek, after which he desired the spectators to bear witness to what he had done. The whole crowd was mute with astonishment, not a murmur more was heard; but they looked upon the two rival champions, and then upon each other with amazement. The high-minded young man had but one course to pursue. Let the consequence be what it might, he could not think for a moment of compromising the character of Ellen, nor of violating his promise, so solemnly given; with a flushed cheek, therefore, and a brow redder even with shame than indignation, he left the crowd without speaking' a word, for he feared that by indulging in any further recrimination on the subject, his resolution might give way under the impetuous resentment which he curbed in with such difficulty.

Meehaul Neil paused and looked after him, equally struck with surprise and contempt at his apparent want of spirit.

"Well," he exclaimed to those who stood about him, "by the life within me, if all the parish had sworn that Lamh Laudher Oge was a coward, I'd not a b'lieved them!"

"Faix, Misther Neil, who would, no more, than yourself?" they replied; "devil the likes of it ever we seen! The young fellow that no man could stand afore five minutes!"

"That is," replied others, "bekase he never met a man that would fight him. You see when he did, how he has turned out. One thing any how is clear enough—after this he can never rise his head while he lives."

CHAPTER III.

Meehaul now directed his steps homewards, literally stunned by the unexpected cowardice of his enemy. On approaching his father's door, he found Nell M'Collum seated on a stone bench, waiting his arrival. The moment she espied him she sprang to her feet, and with her usual eagerness of manner, caught the breast of his coat, and turning him round towards the moonlight, looked eagerly into his face.

"Well," she inquired, "did he show his fire-arms? Well? What was done?"

"Somebody has been making a fool of you, Nell," replied Meehaul; "he had neither fire-arms, nor staff, nor any thing else; an' for my part, I might as well have left mine at home."

"Well, but, *douol*, man, what was done? Did you smash him? Did you break his bones?"

"None of that, Nell, but worse; he's disgraced for ever. I struck him, an' he refused to fight me; he hadn't a hand to raise.

"No! *Dher Chiernah*, he had not; an' he may thank Nell M'Collum for that. I put the weakness over him. But I've not done wid him yet. I'll make that family curse the day they crossed Nell M'Collum, if I should go down for it. Not that I have any ill will to the boy himself, but the father's heart's in him, an' that's the way, Meehaul, I'll punish the man that was the means of lavin' me as I am."

"Nell, the devil's in your heart," replied Meehaul, "if ever he was in mortal's. Lave me, woman: I can't bear your revengeful spirit, an' what is more, I don't want you to interfere in this business, good, bad, or indifferent. You bring about harm, Nell; but who has ever known you to do good?"

"Ay! ay!" said the hag, "that's the cuckoo song to Nell; she does harm, but never does good! Well, may my blackest curse wither the man that left Nell to hear that, as the kindest word that's spoke either to her or of her! I don't blame you. Meehaul—I blame nobody but him for it all. Now a word of advice before you go in; don't let on to

Ellen that you know of her meetin' him this night;—an' reason good,—if she thinks you're watchin' her, she'll be on her guard—'ay, an' outdo you in spite of your teeth. She's a woman—she's a woman. Good night, an' mark him the next time betther."

Meehaul himself—had come to the same determination and from the same motive.

The consciousness of Lamh Laudher's public disgrace, and of his incapability to repel it, sank deep into his heart. The blood in his veins became hot and feverish when he reflected upon the scornful and degrading insult he had just borne. Soon after his return home, his father and mother both noticed the singularly deep bursts of indignant feeling with which he appeared to be agitated. For some time they declined making any inquiry as to its cause, but when they saw at length the big scalding tears of shame and rage start from his flashing eyes, they could no longer restrain their concern and curiosity.

"In the name of heaven, John," said they, "what has happened to put you in such a state as you're in?"

"I can't tell you," he replied; "if you knew it, you'd blush with burnin' shame—you'd curse me in your heart. For my part, I'd rather be dead fifty times over than livin', after what has happened this night."

"An' why not tell us, Lamh Laudher?"

"I can't father; I couldn't stand upright afore you and spake it. I'd sink like a guilty man in your presence; an' except you want to drive me distracted, or perjured, don't ask me another question about it. You'll hear it too soon."

"Well, we must wait," said the father; "but I'm sure, John, you'd not do anything unbecomin' a man. For my part, I'm not unasy on your account, for except to take an affront from a Neil, there's nothing you would do could shame me."

This was a' fresh stab to the son's wounded pride, for which he was not prepared. With a stifled groan he leaped to his feet, and rushing from the kitchen, bolted himself up in his bed-room.

His parents, after he had withdrawn, exchanged glances.

"That went home to him," said the father; "an' as sure as death, the Neils are in it, whatever it is. But by the crass that saved us, if he tuck an affront from any of them, without payin' them home double, he is no son of mine, an' this roof won't cover him another night. Howsomever we'll see in the morn-in', plase God!"

The mother, who was proud of his courage and prowess, scouted with great indignation the idea of her son's tamely putting up with an insult from any of the opposite faction.

"Is it he bear an affront from a Neil! arrah, don't make a fool of yourself, old man! He'd die sooner. I'd stake my life on him."

The night advanced, and the family had retired to bed; but their son attempted in vain to sleep. A sense of shame overpowered him keenly. He tossed and turned, and groaned, at the contemplation of the disgrace which he knew would be heaped on him the following day. What was to be done? How was he to wipe it off? There was but one method, he believed, of getting his hands once more free; that was to seek Ellen, and gain her permission to retract his oath on that very night. With this purpose he instantly dressed, himself, and quietly unbolting his own door, and that of the kitchen, got another staff, and passed out to seek her father's inn.

The night had now become dark, but mild and agreeable; the repose of man and nature was deep, and save his own tumultuous thoughts every thing breathed an air of peace and rest. At a quick but cautious pace he soon reached the inn, and without much difficulty passed into the garden, from which he hoped to be able to make himself known to Ellen. In this, to his great mortification, he was disappointed; the room in which she slept, being on the third story, presented a window, it is true, to the garden; but how was he to reach it, or hold a dialogue with her, even should she recognize him, without being overheard by some of the family? All this might have occurred to him at home, had he been sufficiently cool for reflection. As it was, the only method of awakening her that he could think of was to throw up several handsful of small pebbles against the window. This he tried without any effect. Pebbles sufficiently large to reach the window would have broken the glass, so that he felt himself compelled to abandon every hope of speaking to her that night. With lingering and reluctant steps he left the garden, and stood for some time before the front of the house, leaning against an upright stone, called the market cross. Here he had not been more than two minutes, when he heard footsteps approaching, and on looking closely through the darkness, he recognized the figure of Nell M'Collum, as it passed directly to the kitchen window. Here the crone stopped, peered in, and with caution gave one of the panes a gentle tap. This was responded to by one much louder from within, and almost immediately the door was softly opened. From thence issued another female figure, evidently that of Nanse M'Collum, her niece. Both passed down the street in a northern direction, and Lamh Laudher, apprehensive that they were on no good errand, took off his shoes, lest his footsteps might be heard, and dogged them as they went along. They spoke little, and that in whispers, until they had got clear of the town, when, feeling less restraint, the following dialogue occurred to them:—

"Isn't it a quare thing, aunt, that she should come back to this place at all?"

"Quare enough, but the husband's comin' too—he's to folly her."

"He ought to know that he needn't come here, I think."

"Why, you fool, how do you know that? Sure the town must pay him fifty guineas, if he doesn't get a customer, and that's worth comin' for. She must be near us by this time. Husht! do you hear a car?"

They both paused to listen, but no car was audible.

"I do not," replied the niece; "but isn't it odd that he lets her carry the money, an' him trates her so badly'?"

"Why would it be odd? Sure, she takes betther care of it, an' puts it farther than he does. His heart's in a farden, the nager."

"Rody an' the other will soon spare her that trouble, any way," replied the niece. "Is there no one with her but the carman?"

"Not one—hould you tongue—here's the gate where the same pair was to meet us. Who is this stranger that Rody has picked up? I hope he's the thing."

"Some red-headed fellow. Rody says he is honest. I'm wondherin', aunt, what 'ud happen if she'd know the place."

"She can't, girshah—an' what if she does? She may know the place, but will the place know her? Rody's friend says the best way is to do for her; an' I'm afeard of her, to tell you the truth—but we'll settle that when they come. There now is the gate where we'll sit down. Give a cough till we try if they're———whist! here they are!"

The voices of two men now joined the conversation, but in so low a tone, that Lamh Laudher could not distinctly hear its purport.

The road along which they traveled was craggy, and full of ruts, so that a car could be heard in the silence of night at a considerable distance. On each side the ditches were dry and shallow; and a small elder hedge, which extended its branches towards the road, afforded Lamh Laudher the obscurity which he wanted. With stealthy pace he crept over and sat beneath it, determined to witness whatever incident might occur, and to take a part in it, if necessary. He had scarcely seated himself when the car which they expected was heard jolting about half a mile off along the way, and the next moment a consultation took place in tones so low and guarded, that every attempt on his part to catch its purport was unsuccessful. This continued with much earnestness, if not warmth, until the car came within twenty perches of the gate, when Nell exclaimed—

"If you do, you may—but remember I didn't egg you on, or put it into your hearts, at all evints. Maybe I have a child myself livin'—far from me—an' when I think of him, I feel one touch of nature at my heart in favor of her still. I'm black enough there, as it is."

"Make your mind asy," said one of them, "you won't have to answer for her."

The reply which was given to this could not be heard.

"Well," rejoined, Nell, "I know that. Her comin' here may not be for my good; but—well, take this shawl, an' let the work be quick. The carman must be sent back with sore bones to keep him quiet."

The car immediately reached the spot where they sat, and as it passed, the two men rushed from the gate, stopped the horse, and struck the carman to the earth. One of them seized him while down, and pressed his throat, so as to prevent him from shouting. A single faint shriek escaped the female, who was instantly dragged off the car and gagged by the other fellow and Nanse M'Collum.

Lamh Laudher saw there was not a moment to be lost. With the speed of lightning he sprung forward, and with a single blow laid him who struggled with the carman prostrate. To pass then to the aid of the female was only the work of an instant. With equal success he struck down the villain with whom she was struggling. Such was the rapidity of his motions, that he had not yet had time even to speak; nor indeed did he wish at all to be recognized in the transaction. The carman, finding himself freed from his opponent, bounced to his legs, and came to the assistance of his charge, whilst Lamh Laudher, who had just flung Nanse M'Collum into the ditch, returned in time to defend both from a second attack. The contest, however, was a short one. The two ruffians, finding that there was no chance of succeeding, fled across the fields; and our humble hero, on looking for Nanse and her aunt, discovered that they also had disappeared. It is unnecessary to detail the strong terms in which the strangers expressed their gratitude to Lamh Laudher.

"God's grace be upon you, whoever you are, young man!" exclaimed the carman; "for wid His help an' your own good arm, it's my downright opinion that you saved us from bein' both robbed an' murthered."

"I'm of that opinion myself," replied Lamh Laudher.

"There is goodness, young man, in the tones of your voice," observed the female; "we may at least ask the name of the person who has saved our lives?"

"I would rather not have my name mentioned in the business," he replied; "a woman, or a devil, I think, that I don't wish to cross or provoke, has had a hand in it. I hope you haven't been robbed?" he added.

She assured him, with expressions of deep gratitude, that she had not.

"Well," said he, "as you have neither of you come to much harm, I would take it as the greatest favor you could do me, if you'd never mention a word about it to any one."

To this request they agreed with some hesitation. Lamh Laudher accompanied them into the town, and saw them safely in a decent second-rate inn, kept by a man named Luke Connor, after which he returned to his father's house, and without undressing, fell into a disturbed slumber until morning.

It is not to be supposed that the circumstances attending the quarrel between him and Meehaul Neil, on the preceding night, would pass off without a more than ordinary share of public notice. Their relative positions were too well known not to excite an interest corresponding with the characters they had borne, as the leaders of two bitter and powerful factions: but when it became certain that Meehaul Neil had struck Lamh Laudher Oge, and that the latter refused to fight him, it is impossible to describe the sensation which immediately spread through the town and parish. The intelligence was first received by O'Rorke's party with incredulity and scorn. It was impossible that he of the Strong Hand, who had been proverbial for courage, could all at once turn coward, and bear the blow from a Neil! But when it was proved beyond the possibility of doubt or misconception, that he received a blow tamely before many witnesses, under circumstances of the most degrading insult, the rage of his party became incredible. Before ten o'clock the next morning his father's house was crowded with friends and relations, anxious to hear the truth from his own lips, and all, after having heard it, eager to point out to him the only method that remained of wiping away his disgrace, namely, to challenge Meehaul Neil. His father's indignation knew no bounds; but his mother, on discovering the truth, was not without that pride and love which, are ever ready to form an apology for the feelings and errors of an only child.

"You may all talk," she said; "but if Lamh Laudher Oge didn't strike him, he had good reasons for it. How do you know, an' bad cess to your tongues, all through other, how Ellen Neil would like him after weltin' her brother? Don't ye think she has the spirit of her faction in her as well as another?"

This, however, was not listened to. The father would hear of no apology for his son's cowardice but an instant challenge. Either that or to be driven from his father's roof the only alternatives left him.

"Come out here," said the old man, for the son had not left his humble bed-room, "an' in presence of them that you have brought to shame and disgrace, take the only plan that s left to you, an' send him a challenge."

"Father," said the young man, "I have too much of your own blood in me to be afraid of any man—but for all that, I neither will nor can fight Meehaul Neil."

"Very well," said the father, bitterly, "that's enough. *Dher Manim*, Oonagh, you're a guilty woman; that boy's no son of mine. If he had my blood in him, he couldn't act as he did. Here, you intherloper, the door's open for you; go out of it, an' let me never see the branded face of you while you live." The groans of the son were audible from his bed-room.

"I will go, father," he replied, "an' I hope the day will come when you'll all change your opinion of me. I can't, however, stir out till I send a message a mile or so out of town."

The old man in the mean time, wept as if his son had been dead; his tears, however, were not those of sorrow, but of shame and indignation.

"How can I help it," he exclaimed, "when I think of the way that the Neils will clap their wings and crow over us! If it was from any other family he tuck it so inanely, I wouldn't care so much; but from them! Oh, Chiernah! it's too bad! Turn out, you villain!"

A charge of deeper disgrace, however, awaited the unhappy young man. The last harsh words of the father had scarcely been uttered, when three constables came in, and inquired if his son were at home.

"He is at home," said the father, with tears in his eyes, "and I never thought he would bring the blush to my face as he did by his conduct last night."

"I am sorry," said the principal of them, "for what has happened, both on your account and his. Do you know this hat?"

"I do know it," replied the old man; "it belongs to John. Come out here," said he, "here's Tom Breen wid your hat."

The son left his room, and it was evident from his appearance that he had not undressed at all during the night. The constables immediately observed these circumstances, which they did not fail to interpret to his disadvantage.

"Here is your hat," said the man who bore it; "one would think you were travelin' all night, by your looks."

The son thanked him for his civility, got clean stockings, and after arranging his dress, said to his father—

"I'm now ready to go, father, an' as I can't do what you want me to do, there's nothing for me but to leave the country for a while."

"He acknowledged it himself," said the father, turning to Breen; "an' in that case, how could I let the son that shamed me live undher my roof?"

"He's the last young man in the country I stand in," said Breen, "that any one who knew him would suspect to be guilty of robbery. Upon my soul, Lamh Laudher More, I'm both grieved an' distressed at it. We're come to arrest him," he added, "for the robbery he committed last night."

"Robbery!" they exclaimed with one voice.

"Ay," said the man, "robbery, no less—an' what is more, I'm afraid there's little doubt of his guilt. Why did he lave his hat at the place where the attempt was first made? He must come with us."

The mother shrieked aloud, and clapped her hands like a distressed woman; the father's brow changed from the flushed hue of indignation, and became pale with apprehension.

"Oh! no, no," he exclaimed, "John never did that. Some qualm might come over him in the other business, but—no, no—your father knows you're innocent of robbery. Yes, John, my blood is in you, and there you're wronged, my son. I know you too well, in spite of all I've said to you, to believe that, my true-hearted boy."

He grasped his son's hand as he spoke.

And his mother at the same moment caught him in her arms, whilst both sobbed aloud. A strong sense of innate dignity expanded the brow of young Lamh Laudher. He smiled while his parents wept, although his sympathy in their sorrow brought a tear at the same time to his eye-lids. He declined, however, entering into any explanation, and the father proceeded—

"Yes! I know you are innocent, John; I can swear that you didn't leave this house from nine o'clock last night up to the present minute."

"Father," said Lamh Laudher, "don't swear that, for it would not be true, although you think it would. I was out the greater part of last night."

His father's countenance fell again, as did those of his friends who were present, on hearing what appeared to be almost an admission of his guilt.

"Go," said the old man, "go; naburs, take him with you. If he's guilty of this, I'll never more look upon his face. John, my heart was crushed before, but you're likely to break it out an' out."

Lamh Laudher Oge's deportment, on hearing himself charged with robbery, became dogged and sullen. The conversation, together with the sympathy and the doubt it excited among his friends, he treated with silent indignation and scorn. He remembered that on the night before, the strange woman assured him she had not been robbed, and he felt that the charge was exceedingly strange and unaccountable.

"Come," said he, "the sooner this business is cleared up the better. For my part, I don't know what to make of it, nor do I care much how it goes. I knew since yesterday evening, that bad luck was before me, at all events, an' I suppose it must take its course, an' that I must bear it."

The father had sat down, and now declined uttering a single word in vindication of his' son. The latter looked towards him, when about to pass out, but the old man waved his hand with sorrowful impatience, and pointed to the door, as intimating a wish that he should forthwith depart from under his roof. Loaded with twofold disgrace, he left his family and his friends, accompanied by the constables, to the profound grief and astonishment of all who knew him.

They then conducted him before a Mr. Brooldeigh, an active magistrate of that day, and a gentleman of mild and humane character.

CHAPTER IV.

On reaching Brookleigh Hall, Lamh Laudher found the strange woman, Nell M'Collum, Connor's servant maid, and the carman awaiting his arrival. The magistrate looked keenly at the prisoner, and immediately glanced with an expression of strong disgust at Nell M'Collum. The other female surveyed Lamh Laudher with an interest evidently deep; after which she whispered something to Nell, who frowned and shook her head, as if dissenting from what she had heard. Lamh Laudher, on his part surveyed the features of the female with an earnestness that seemed to absorb all sense of his own disgrace and danger.

"O'Rorke," said the magistrate, "this is a serious charge against you. I trust you may be able effectually to meet it."

"I must wait, your worship, till I hear fully what it is first," replied Lamh Laudher, "afther that I'm not afraid of clearin' myself from it."

The woman then detailed the circumstances of the robbery, which it appeared took place at the moment her luggage was in the act of being removed to her room, after which she added, rather unexpectedly—"And now your worship, I have plainly stated the facts; but I must, in conscience, add, that although this woman," turning to Nell M'Collum, "is of opinion that the young man before you has robbed me, yet I cannot think he did."

"I'll swear, your worship," said Nell, "that on passin' homewards last night, seein' a car wid people about it, at Luke Connor's door, I stood behind the porch, merely to thry if I knew who they wor. I seen this Lamh Laudher wid a small oak box in his hands, an' I'll give my oath that it was open, an' that he put his hands into it, and tuck something out."

"Pray, Nell, how did it happen that you yourself were abroad at so unseasonable an hour?" said the magistrate.

"Every one knows that I'm out at quare hours," replied Nell; "I'm not like others. I know where I ought to be, at all times; but last night, if your worship wishes to hear the truth, I was on my way to Andy Murray's wake, the poor lad that was shepherd to the Neils."

The Dead Boxer

"And pray, Nell," said his worship, "how did you form so sudden an acquaintance with this respectable looking woman?"

"I knew her for years," said Nell; "I've seen her in other parts of the country often."

"You were more than an hour with her last night—were you not?" said his worship.

"She made me stay wid her," said Nell, "bekase she was a stranger, an' of coorse was glad to see a face she know, afther the fright she got."

"All very natural, Nell; but in the mean time, she might easily have chosen a more respectable associate. Have you actually lost the sum of six hundred pounds, my good madam?"

"I have positively lost so much," replied the woman, "together with the certificate of my marriage."

"And how did you become acquainted with Nell M'Collum?" he inquired.

The stranger was silent, and blushed deeply at this question; but Nell, with more presence of mind, went over to the magistrate, and whispered something which caused him to start, look keenly at her, and then at the plaintiff.

"I must have this confirmed by herself" he said in reply to Nell's disclosure, "otherwise I shall be much more inclined to consider you the thief than O'Rorke, whose character has been hitherto unimpeachable and above suspicion."

He then beckoned the woman over to his desk, and after having first inquired if she could write, and being replied to in the affirmative, he placed a slip of paper before her, on which was written—"Is that unhappy woman called Nell M'Collum, your mother?"

"Alas! she is, sir," replied the female, with a deep expression of sorrow. The magistrate then appeared satisfied. "Now," said he, addressing O'Rorke, "state, fairly and honestly what you have to say in reply to the charge brought against you."

"Please your worship," said the young man, "you hear the woman say that she brings no charge against me; but I can prove on oath, that Nell M'Collum and her niece, Nanse M'Collum, along with two men that I don't know, except that one was called Rody, met at Franklin's gate, with an intention of robing, an' it's my firm belief, of murdering this woman."

He then detailed with great earnestness the incidents and conversation of the preceding night.

"Sir," replied Nell, with astonishing promptness, "I can prove by two witnesses, that, no longer ago than last night, he said he would take to the high-road, in ordher to get money to enable him to marry Ellen Neil. Yes, you villain, Nanse M'Collum heard every word that passed between you and her in the grassy quarry; an' Ellen, your worship, can prove it too, if she's sent for."

This had little effect on the magistrate, who at no time placed any reliance on Nell's assertions; he immediately, however, dispatched a summons for Nanse M'Collum.

The carman then related all that he knew, every word of which strongly corroborated what Lamh Laudher had said. He concluded by declaring it to be his opinion, that the prisoner was innocent, and added, that, according to the best of his belief, the box was not open when he left it in the plaintiff's sleeping-room above stairs.

The magistrate again looked keenly and suspiciously towards Nell. At this stage of the proceedings, O'Rorke's father and mother, accompanied by some of their friends, made their appearance. The old man, however, declined to take any part in the vindication of his son. He stood sullenly silent, with his arms folded and his brows knit, as much in indignation as in sorrow. The grief of the mother was louder, for she wept audibly.

Ere the lapse of many minutes, the constable returned, and stated that Nanse was not be found.

"She has not been at her master's house since morning," he observed, "and they don't know where she is, or what has become of her."

The magistrate immediately despatched two of the constables, with strict injunctions! to secure her, if possible.

"In the mean time," he added, "I will order you, Nell M'Collum, to be strictly confined, until I ascertain whether she can be produced or not. Your haunts may be searched with some hope of success, while you are in durance; but I rather think we might seek for her in vain, if you were at liberty to regulate her motions. I cannot expect," he added, turning to the stranger, "that you should prosecute one so nearly related to you, even if you had proof, which you have not; but I am almost certain, that she has been someway or other concerned in the robbery. You are a modest, interesting woman, and I regret the loss you have sustained. At present there are no grounds for committing any of the parties charged with the robbery. This unhappy woman I commit only as a vagrant, until her niece is found, after that we shall probably be able to see somewhat farther into this strange affair."

"Something tells' me, sir," replied the stranger, "that this young man is as innocent of the robbery as the child unborn. It's not my intention ever to think of prosecuting him. What I have done in the matter was against my own wishes."

"God in heaven bless you for the words!" exclaimed the parents of O'Rorke, each pressing her hand with delight and gratitude. The woman warmly returned their greetings, but instantly felt her bosom heave with a hysterical oppression under which she sank into a state of insensibility. Lamh Laudher More and his wife were proceeding to bring her towards the door for air, when Nell M'Collum insisted on a prior right to render her that service. "Begone, you servant of the devil," exclaimed the old man, "your wicked breath is bad about any one else; you won!t lay a hand upon her."

"Don't let her, for heaven's sake!" said his wife; "her eye will kill the woman!"

"You are not aware," said the magistrate, "that this woman is her daughter?"

"Whose daughter, please your honor," said the old man indignantly.

"Nell M'Collum's," he returned.

"It's as false as hell!" rejoined O'Rorke, "beggin' your honor's pardon for sayin' so. I mean it's false for Nell, if she says it. Nell, sir, never had a daughter, an' she knows that; but she had a son, an' she knows best what became of him."

Nell, however, resolved not to be deterred from getting-the stranger into her own hands. With astonishing strength and fury she attempted to drag the insensible creature from O'Rorke's grasp; but the magistrate, disgusted at her violence, ordered two of the persons present to hold her down.

At length the woman began to recover.

She sobbed aloud, and a copious flow of tears drenched her cheeks. Nell ordered her to tear herself from O'Rorke and his wife:— "Their hands are bad about you," she exclaimed, "and their son has robbed you, Mary. Lave them, I say, or it will be worse for you."

The woman paid her no attention; on the contrary, she laid her head on the bosom of O'Rorke's wife, and wept as if her heart would break.

"God help me!" she exclaimed with a bitter sense of her situation, "I am an unhappy, an' a heart-broken woman! For many a year I have not known what it is to have a friendly breast to weep on."

She then caught O'Rorke's hand and kissed it affectionately, after which she wept afresh;

"Merciful heaven!" said she'—"oh, how will I ever be able to meet my husband! and such a husband! oh, heavens pity me!"

Both O'Rorke and his wife stood over her in tears. The latter bent her head, kissed the stranger, and pressed her to her bosom. "May God bless you!" said O'Rorke himself solemnly; "trust in Him, for he can see justice done to you when man fails."

The eyes of Nell glared at the group like those of an enraged tigress: she stamped her feet upon the floor, and struck it repeatedly with her stick, as she was in the habit of doing, when moved by strong and deadly passions.

"You'll suffer for that, Mary," she exclaimed; "and as for you, Lamh Laudher More, my debt's not paid to you yet. Your son's a robber, an I'll prove it before long; every one knows he's a coward too."

Mr. Brookleigh felt that there appeared to be something connected with the transactions of the preceding night, as well as with some of the persons who had come before him, that perplexed him not a little. He thought that, considering the serious nature of the charge preferred against young O'Rorke, he exhibited an apathy under it, that did not altogether argue innocence. Some unsettled suspicions entered his mind, but not with sufficient force to fix with certainty upon any of those present, except Nell and Nanse M'Collum who had absconded. If Nell were the woman's mother, her anxiety to bring the criminal to justice appeared very natural. Then, again, young O'Rorke's father, who seemed to know the history of Nell M'Collum, denied that she ever had a daughter. How could he be certain that she had not, without knowing her private life thoroughly? These circumstances appeared rather strange, if not altogether incomprehensible; so much so, indeed, that he thought it necessary, before they separated, to speak with O'Rorke's family in private. Having expressed a wish to this effect, he dismissed the other parties, except Nell, whom he intended to keep confined until the discovery of her niece.

"Pray," said he to the father of our humble hero, "how do you know, O'Rorke, that Nell M'Collum never had a daughter?"

"Right well, your honor. I knew her since she was a child; an' from that day to this she was never six months from this town at a time. No, no—a son she had, but a daughter she never had."

"Let me ask you, young man, on what business were you abroad last night? I expect you will answer me candidly?"

"It's no matter," replied young Lamh Laudher gloomily, "my character's gone. I cannot be worse, an' I will tell no man how I spent it, till I have an opportunity of clarin' myself."

"If you spent it innocently," returned the magistrate, "you can have no hesitation in making the disclosure we require."

"I will not mention it," said the other; "I was disgraced, an' that is enough. I think but little of the robbery."

Brookleigh understood him; but the last assertion, though it exonerated him in the opinion of a man who knew something about character, went far in that of his friends who were present to establish his guilt.

They then withdrew; and it would have been much to young Lamh Laudher's advantage if this private interview had never taken place.

CHAPTER V.

The next morning O'Rorke and his wife! waited upon Mr. Brookleigh to state, that in their opinion it would be more judicious to liberate Nell M'Collum, provided he kept a strict watch upon all her motions. The magistrate instantly admitted both the force and ingenuity of the thought; and after having appointed three persons to the task of keeping her under surveillance, he set her at large.

This was all judicious and prudent; but in the mean time, common rumor, having first published the fact of young Lamh Laudher's cowardice, found it an easy task to associate his name with the robbery. His very father, after their last conference with the magistrate, doubted him; his friends, in the most sympathetic terms, expressed their conviction of his guilt, and the natural consequence resulting from this was, that he found himself expelled from his paternal roof, and absolutely put out of caste. The tide of ill-fame, in fact, set in so strongly against him, that Ellen, startled as she had been by his threat of taking to the highway, doubted him. The poor young man, in truth, led a miserable life. Nanse M'Collum had not been found, and the unfavorable rumor was still at its height, when one morning the town arose and found the walls and streets placarded with what was in those days known as the fatal challenge of the DEAD BOXER!

This method of intimating his arrival had always been peculiar to that individual, who was a man of color. No person ever discovered the means by which he placarded his dreadful challenge. In an age of gross superstition, numerous were the rumors and opinions promulgated concerning this circumstance. The general impression was, that an evil spirit attended him, by whose agency his advertisements were put up at night; A law, it is said, then existed, that when a pugilist arrived in any town, He might claim the right to receive the sum of fifty guineas, provided no man in the town could be found to accept his challenge within a given period. A champion, if tradition be true, had the privilege of fixing only the place, not the mode and regulations of battle. Accordingly the scene of contest uniformly selected by the Dead Boxer was the church-yard of the town, beside a new made grave, dug at his expense. The epithet of the Dead Boxer had been given to him, in consequence of a certain fatal stroke by which he had been able to kill every antagonist who dared to meet him; precisely on the same principle that we call a fatal marksman a dead shot; and the church-yard was selected, and the grave prepared, in order to denote the fatality incurred by those who went into a contest with him. He was famous, too, at athletic sports, but was never known to communicate the secret of the fatal blow; he also taught the sword exercises, at which he was considered to be a proficient.

On the morning after his arrival, the town in which we have laid the scene of this legend felt the usual impulse of an intense curiosity to see so celebrated a character. The Dead Boxer, however, appeared to be exceedingly anxious to gratify this natural propensity. He walked out from the head inn, where he had stopped, attended by his servant, merely, it would appear, to satisfy them as to the very slight chance which the stoutest of them had in standing before a man whose blow was so fatal, and whose frame so prodigiously Herculean.

Twelve o'clock was the hour at which he deemed proper to make his appearance, and as it happened also to be the market-day of the town, the crowd which followed him was unprecedented. The old and young, the hale and feeble of both sexes, all rushed out to see, with feelings of fear and wonder, the terrible and far-famed Dead Boxer. The report of his arrival had already spread far and wide into the country, and persons belonging to every class and rank of life might be seen hastening on horseback, and more at full speed on foot, that they might, if possible, catch an early glimpse of him. The most sporting characters among the nobility and gentry of the country, fighting-peers, fire-eaters, snuff-candle squires, members of the hell-fire and jockey clubs, gaugers, gentlemen tinners, bluff yeomen, laborers, cudgel-players, parish pugilists, men of renown within a district of ten square miles, all jostled each other in hurrying to see, and if possible to have speech of, the Dead Boxer. Not a word was spoken that day, except with reference to him, nor a conversation introduced, the topic of which was not the Dead Boxer. In the town every window was filled with persons standing to get a view of him; so were the tops of the houses, the dead walls, and all the cars, gates, and available eminences within sight of the way along which he went. Having thus perambulated the town, he returned to the market-cross, which, as we have said, stood immediately in front of his inn. Here, attended by music, he personally published his challenge in a deep and sonorous voice, calling upon the corporation in right of his championship, to produce a man in ten clear days ready to undertake battle with him as a pugilist, or otherwise to pay him the sum of fifty guineas out of their own proper exchequer.

Having thus thrown down his gauntlet, the musicians played a dead march, and there was certainly something wild and fearful in the association produced by these strains of death and the fatality of encountering him. This challenge he repeated at the same place and hour during three successive days, after which he calmly awaited the result.

In the mean time, certain circumstances came to light, which not only developed many cruel and profligate traits in his disposition, but also enabled the worthy inhabitants of the town to ascertain several facts relating to his connections, which in no small degree astonished them. The candid and modest female whose murder and robbery had been planned by Nell M'Collum, resided with him as his wife; at least if he did not acknowledge her as such, no person who had an opportunity of witnessing her mild and gentle deportment, ever for a moment conceived her capable of living with him in any other character, his conduct to her, however, was brutal in the extreme, nor was his open and unmanly cruelty lessened by the misfortune of her having lost the money which he had accumulated. With Nell M'Collum he was also acquainted, for he had given orders that she should be admitted to him whenever she deemed it necessary. Nell, though now at large, found her motions watched with a vigilance which no ingenuity on her part, could baffle. She knew this, and was resolved by caution to overreach those who dogged her so closely. Her intimacy with the Dead Boxer threw a shade of still deeper mystery around her own character and his. Both were supposed to be capable of entering into evil communion with supernatural beings, and both, of course, were looked upon with fear and hatred, modified, to be sure, by the peculiarity of their respective situations.

Let not our readers, however, suppose that young Lamh Laudher's disgrace was altogether lost in the wide-spread fame of the Dead Boxer. His high reputation for generous and manly feeling had given him too strong a hold upon the hearts of all who know him, to be at once discarded by them from public conversation as an indifferent person. His conduct filled them with wonder, it is true; but although the general tone of feeling respecting the robbery was decidedly in his favor, yet there still existed among the public, particularly in the faction that was hostile to him, enough of doubt, openly expressed, to render it a duty to avoid him; particularly when this formidable suspicion was joined to the notorious fact of his cowardice in the rencounter with Meehaul Neil. Both subjects were therefore discussed with probably an equal interest; but it is quite certain that the rumor of Lamh Laudher's cowardice would alone have occasioned him, under the peculiar circumstances which drew it forth, to be avoided and branded with contumely. There was, in fact, then in existence among the rival factions in Ireland much of the military sense of honor which characterizes the British army at this day; nor is this spirit even yet wholly exploded, from our humble countrymen. Poor Lamh Laudher was, therefore, an exile from his father's house, repulsed and avoided by all who had formerly been intimate with him.

There was another individual, however, who deeply sympathized in all he felt, because she knew that for her sake it had been incurred; we allude to Ellen Neil. Since the night of their last interview, she, too, had been scrupulously watched by her relations. But what vigilance can surpass the ingenuity of love? Although her former treacherous confidant had absconded, yet the incident of the Dead Boxer's arrival had been the means of supplying her with a friend, into whose bosom she felt that she could pour out all the anxieties of her heart. This was no other than the Dead Boxer's wife; and there was this peculiarity in the interest which she took in Ellen's distress, that it was only a return of sympathy which Ellen felt in the unhappy woman's sufferings. The conduct of her husband was indefensible; for while he treated her with shameful barbarity, it was evident that his bad passions and his judgment were at variance, with respect to the estimate which he formed of her character. In her honesty he placed every confidence, and permitted her to manage his money and regulate his expenses; but this was merely because her frugality and economic habits gratified his parsimony, and fostered one of his strongest passions, which was avarice. There was something about this amiable creature that won powerfully upon the affections of Ellen Neil; and in entrusting her with the secret of her love, she she felt assured that she had not misplaced it. Their private conversations, therefore, were frequent, and their communications, unreserved on both sides, so far as woman can bestow confidence and friendship on the subject of her affections or her duty. This intimacy did not long escape the prying eyes of Nell M'Collum, who soon took means to avail herself of it for purposes which will shortly become evident.

It was about the sixth evening after the day on which the Dead Boxer had published his challenge, that, having noticed Nell from a window as she passed the inn, he dispatched a waiter with a message that she should be sent up to him. Previous to this the hag had been several times with his wife, on whom she laid serious injunctions never to disclose to her husband the relationship between them. The woman had never done so, for in fact the acknowledgement of Nell, as her mother, would have been to, any female whose feelings had not been made callous by the world, a painful and distressing task. Nell was the more anxious on this point, as she feared that such a disclosure would have frustrated her own designs.

"Well, granny," said he, when Nell entered, "any word of the money?"

Nell cautiously shut the door, and stood immediately fronting him, her hand at some distance from her side, supported by her staff, and her gray glittering eyes fixed upon him with that malicious look which she never could banish from her countenance.

"The money will come," she replied, "in good time. I've a charm near ready that'll get a clue to it. I'm watchin' him—and I'm watched myself—an' Ellen's watched. He has hardly a house to put his head in; but *nabockish!* I'll bring you an' him together—ay, *dher manim*, an'

I'll make him give you the first blow; afther that, if you don't give him one, it's your own fau't."

"Get the money first, granny. I won't give him the blow till *it* is safe."

"Won't you?" replied the beldame; "ay, *dher Creestha*, will you, whin you know what. I have to tell you about him an'—an'——"

"And who, granny?"

"*Diououl*, man, but I'm afeard to tell you, for fraid you'd kill me."

"Tut, Nelly; I'd not strike an Obeah-wo-man," said he, laughing.

"I suspect foul play between him an'—her."

"Eh? Fury of hell, no!"

"He's very handsome," said the other, "an' young—far younger than you are, by thirteen—"

"Go on—go on," said the Dead Boxer, interrupting her, and clenching his fist, whilst his eyes literally glowed like live coals, "go on—I'll murder him, but not till—yes, I'll murder him at a blow—I will; but no—not till you secure the money first. If I give him the blow—THE BOX—I might never get it, granny. A dead man gives back nothing."

"I suspect," replied Nell, "*arraghid*—that is the money—is in other hands. Lord presarve us! but it's a wicked world, blackey."

"Where is it!" said the Boxer, with a vehemence of manner resembling that of a man who was ready to sink to perdition for his wealth. "Devil! and furies! where is it?"

"Where is it?" said the imperturbable Nell; "why, manim a yeah, man, sure you don't think that I know where it is? I suspect that your landlord's daughter, his real sweetheart, knows something about it; but thin, you see, I can prove nothing; I only suspect. We must watch an' wait. You know she wouldn't prosecute him."

"We will watch an' wait—but I'll finish him. Tell me, Nell—fury of hell, woman—can it be possible—no—well—I'll murder him, though; but can it be possible that she's guilty? eh? She wouldn't prosecute him—No—no—she would not."

The Dead Boxer

"She is not worthy of you, blackey. Lord save us! Well, troth, I remimber whin you wor in Lord S—'s, you were a fine young man of your color. I did something for the young lord in my way then, an' I used to say, when I called to see her, that you wor a beauty, barrin' the face. Sure enough, there was no lie in that. Well, that was before you tuck to the fightin'; but I'm ravin'. Whisper, man. If you doubt what I'm sayin', watch the north corner of the orchard about nine tonight, an' you'll see a meetin' between her an' O'Rorke. God be wid you! I must go."

"Stop!" said the Boxer; "don't—but do get a charm for the money."

"Good-by," said Nell; "*you* a heart wid your money! No; *damnho sherry* on the charm ever I'll get you till you show more spunk. You! My curse on the money, man, when your disgrace is consarned!"

Nell passed rapidly, and with evident indignation out of the room; nor could any entreaty on the part of the Dead Boxer induce her to return and prolong the dialogue.

She had said enough, however, to produce in his bosom torments almost equal to those of the damned. In several of their preceding dialogues, she had impressed him with a belief that young Lamh Laudher was the person who had robbed his wife; and now to the hatred that originated in a spirit of avarice, she added the deep and deadly one of jealousy. On the other hand, the Dead Boxer had, in fact, begun to feel the influence of Ellen Neil's beauty; and perhaps nothing would have given him greater satisfaction than the removal of a woman whom he no longer loved, except for those virtues which enabled him to accumulate money. And now, too, had he an equal interest in the removal of his double rival, whom, besides, he considered the spoliator of his hoarded property. The loss of this money certainly stung him to the soul, and caused his unfortunate wife to suffer a tenfold degree of persecution and misery. When to this we add his sudden passion for Ellen Neil, we may easily conceive what she must have endured. Nell, at all events, felt satisfied that she had shaped the strong passions of her savage dupe in the way best calculated to gratify that undying spirit of vengeance which she had so long nurtured against the family of Lamh Laudher. The Dead Boxer, too, was determined to prosecute his amour with

The Dead Boxer

Ellen Neil, not more to gratify his lawless affection for her than his twofold hatred of Lamh Laudher.

At length nine o'clock arrived, and the scene must change to the northern part of Sheemus Neil's orchard. The Dead Boxer threw a cloak around him, and issuing through the back door of the inn, entered the garden, which was separated from the orchard only by a low clipped hedge of young whitethorn, in the middle of which stood of a small gate. In a moment he was in the orchard, and from behind its low wall he perceived a female proceeding to the north side muffled like himself in a cloak, which he immediately recognized to be that of his wife. His teeth became locked together with the most deadly resentment; his features twitched with the convulsive spasms of rage, and his nostrils were distended as if his victims stood already within his grasp. He instantly threw himself over the wall, and nothing but the crashing weight of his tread could have saved the lives of the two unsuspecting persons before him. Startled, however, by the noise of his footsteps, Lamh Laudher turned round to observe who it was that followed them, and immediately the massy and colossal black now stripped of his cloak—for he had thrown it aside—stood in their presence. The female instinctively drew the cloak round her face, and Lamh Laudher was about to ask why he followed them, when the Boxer approached him in an attitude of assault.

With a calmness almost unparalleled under the circumstances, Lamh Laudher desired the female by no means to cling to him.

"If you do," said he, "I am murdered where I stand."

"No," she shrieked, "you shall not. Stand back, man, stand back, if you murder him I will take care you shall suffer for it. Stand back. Lamh Laudher never injured you."

"Ha!" exclaimed the Boxer, in reply; "why, what is this! Who have we here?"

Ellen, for it was she, had already thrown back the cloak from her features, and stepped forward between them.

"Well, I am glad it is you," said the black, "and so may he. Come, I shall conduct you home."

The Dead Boxer

He caught her arm as he spoke, and drew her over to his side like an infant.

"Come, my pretty girl, come; I will treat you tenderly, and all I shall ask is a kiss in return. Here, young fellow," said he to Lamh Laudher, with a sense of bitter triumph, "I will show you that one black kiss is worth two white ones."

Heavy, hard, and energetic was the blow which the Dead Boxer received upon the temple, as the reply of Lamh Laudher, and dead was the crash of his tremendous body on the earth. Ellen looked around her with amazement.

"Come," said she, seizing her lover's arm, and dragging him onward: "gracious heavens! I hope you haven't killed him. Come, John, the time is short, and we must make the most of it. That villain, as I tould you before, is a villain. Oh! if you knew it! John, I have been the manes of your disgrace and suffering, but I am willing to do what I can to remedy that. In your disgrace, Ellen will be ready, in four days from this, to become your wife. John, come to meet me no more. I will send that villain's innocent wife to your aunt Alley's, where you now live'. I didn't expect to see you myself; but I got an opportunity, and besides she was too unwell to bring my message, which was to let you know what I now tell you."

John, ere he replied, looked behind him at the Dead Boxer, and appeared as if struck with some sudden thought.

"He is movin'," said he, "an' on this night I don't wish to meet him again; but—yes, Ellen, yes—God bless you for the words you've said; but how could you for one minute doubt me about the robbery?"

"I did not, John—I did not; and if I did, think of your own words at our meetin' in the Quarry; it was a small suspicion, though—no more. No, no; at heart I never doubted you."

"Ellen," said John, "hear me. You never will become my wife till my disgrace is wiped away. I love you too well ever to see you blush for your husband. My mind's made up—so say no more. Ay, an' I tell you that to live three months in this state would break my heart."

"Poor John!" she exclaimed, as they separated, and the words were followed by a gush of tears, "I know that there is not one of them, in either of the factions, so noble in heart and thought as you are."

"Ill prove that soon, Ellen; but never till my name is fair and clear, an' without spot, can you be my wife. Good night, dearest; in every thing but that I'll be guided by you."

They then separated, and immediately the Dead Boxer, like a drunken man, went tottering, rather crest-fallen, towards the inn. On reaching his own room, his rage appeared quite ungovernable; he stormed, stamped, and raved on reflecting that any one was able to knock him down. He called for brandy and water, with a curse to the waiter, swore deeply between every sip, and, ultimately dispatched another messenger for Nell M'Collum.

"That Obeah woman's playing on me," he exclaimed; "because my face is black, she thinks me a fool. Furies! I neither know what she is, nor who the other is. But I will know."

"Don't be too sure of that," replied Nell, gliding into the apartment— "You can say little, blackey, or think little, avourneen, that I'll not know. As to who she is, you needn't ax—she won't be long troublin' you; an' in regard to myself, I'm what you see me. Arra, *dher ma chuirp*, man alive, I could lave you in one night that a boy in his first *breestha* (small clothes) could bate the marrow out of you."

"Where did you come from now, granny?"

"From her room; she's sick—that was what prevented her from meetin' Lamh Laudher."

"Granny, do you know who she is? I'm tired of her—sick of her."

"You know enough about her to satisfy you. Wasn't she a beautiful creature when Lady S——— tuck her into the family, an' reared her till she was fit to wait upon herself. Warn't you then sarvant to the ould lord, an' didn't I make her marry you, something against her will, too; but she did it to plase me. That was before 'buildin' churches' druv you out of the family, an' made you take to the fightin' trade."

"Granny, you must bring this young fellow across me. Blood! woman, do you know what he did? He knocked me down, granny—struck me senseless! Fury of hell! Me! Only for attempting to kiss his sweetheart!"

"Ha!" said Nell, bitterly, "keep that to yourself, for heaven's sake! *Dher ma chuirp*, man, if it was known, his name would be higher up than ever. Be my sowl, any how, that was the Lamh Laudher blow, my boy, an' what that is, is well known. The devil curse him for it!"

"Granny, you must assist me in three things. Find a clue to the money—bring this fellow in my way, as you promised—and help me with the landlord's daughter."

"Is there nothin' else?"

"What?"

"She's sick."

"Well, let her die, then; I don't care."

"In the other things I will help you," said Nell; "but you must clear your own way there. I can do every thing but that. I have a son myself, an' my hands is tied against blood till I find him out. I could like to see some people withered, but I can't kill."

"Well, except her case, we understand one another. Good night, then."

"You must work that for yourself. Good night."

CHAPTER VI.

In the mean time a circumstance occurred which scarcely any person who heard it could at first believe. About twelve o'clock the next day the house of Lamh Laudher More was surrounded with an immense crowd, and the whole town seemed to be in a state of peculiar animation and excitement. Groups met, stood, and eagerly accosted each other upon some topic that evidently excited equal interest and astonishment.

LAMH LAUDHER OGE HAD CHALLENGED THE DEAD BOXER.

True. On that morning, at an early hour, the proscribed young man waited upon the Sovereign of the town, and requested to see him. Immediately after his encounter with the black the preceding night, and while Ellen Neil offered to compensate him for the obloquy she had brought upon his name, he formed the dreadful resolution of sending him a challenge. In very few words he stated his intention to the Sovereign, who looked upon him as insane.

"No, no," replied that gentleman; "go home, O'Rorke, and banish the idea out of your head; it is madness."

"But I say yes, yes, with great respect to you, sir," observed Lamh Laudher. "I've been banished from my father's house, and treated with scorn by all that know me, because they think me a coward. Now I'll let them know I'm no coward."

"But you will certainly be killed," said, the Sovereign.

"That's to be seen," observed the young man; "at all events, I'd as soon be killed as livin' in disgrace. I'll thank you, sir, as the head of the town, to let the black know that Lamh Laudher Oge will fight him."

"For heaven's sake, reflect a moment upon the— —"

"My mind's made up to fight," said the other, interrupting him. "No power on earth will prevent me, sir. So, if you don't choose to send the challenge, I'll bring it myself."

The Sovereign shook his head, as if conscious of what the result must be.

"That is enough," said he; "as you are fixed on your own destruction, the challenge will be given; but I trust you will think better of it."

"Let him know, if you please," added Lamh Laudher, "that on to-morrow at twelve o'clock we must fight."

The magistrate nodded, and Lamh Laudher immediately took his leave. In a short time the intelligence spread. From the sovereign it passed to his clerk, from the clerk to the other members of the corporation, and, ere an hour, the town was in a blaze with the intelligence.

"Did you hear what's reported?" was the general question.

Lamh Laudher Oge has challenged the Dead Boxer!

The reader already knows how bitterly public opinion had set in against our humble hero; but it would be difficult to describe, in terms sufficiently vivid, the rapid and powerful reaction which now took place in his favor. Every one pitied him, praised him, remembered his former prowess, and after finding some palliative for his degrading interview with Meehaul Neil, concluded with expressing a firm conviction that he had undertaken a fatal task. When the rumor had reached his parents, the blood ran cold in their veins, and their natural affection, now roused into energy, grasped at an object that was about to be violently removed from it. Their friends and neighbors, as we have stated, came to their house for the purpose of dissuading their son against so rash and terrible an undertaking.

"It musn't be," said they, "for whatever was over him wid Meehaul Neil, we know now he's no coward, an' that's enough. We musn't see him beat dead before our eyes, at all events, where is he?"

"He's at his aunt's," replied the father; "undher this roof he says he will never come till his name is cleared. Heavens above! For him to think of fighting a man that kills every one he fights wid!"

The Dead Boxer

The mother's outcries were violent, as were those of his female relations, whilst a solemn and even mournful spirit brooded upon the countenances of his own faction. It was resolved that his parents and friends should now wait upon, and by every argument and remonstrance in their power, endeavor to change the rashness of his purpose:

The young man received them with a kind but somewhat sorrowful, spirit. The father, uncovered, and with his gray locks flowing down upon his shoulders, approached him, extended his hand, and with an infirm voice said—

"Give me your hand, John. You're welcome to your father's heart an' your father's roof once more."

The son put his arms across his breast, and bowed his head respectfully, but declined receiving his father's hand.

"Not, father—father dear—not till my name is cleared."

"John," said the old man, now in tears, "will you refuse me? You are my only son, my only child, an' I cannot lose you. Your name is cleared."

"Father," said the son, "I've sworn—it's now too late. My heart, father, has been crushed by what has happened lately. I found little charity among my friend's. I say, I cannot change my mind, for I've sworn to fight him. And even if I had not sworn, I couldn't, as a man, but do it, for he has insulted them that I love better than my own life. I knew you would want to persuade me against what I'm doin'—an' that was why I bound myself this mornin' by an oath."

The mother, who had been detained a few minutes behind them, now entered, and on hearing that he had refused to decline the battle, exclaimed—

"Who says that Lamh Laudher Oge won't obey his mother? Who dare say it? Wasn't he ever and always an obedient son to me an' his father? I won't believe that lie of my boy, no more than I ever believed a word of' what was sed against him. *Shawn Oge aroon*, you won't refuse me, *avillish*. What 'ud become of me, *avich ma chree*, if you fight him? Would you have the mother's heart broken, an' our roof childless all out? We lost one as it is—the daughter of our heart

The Dead Boxer

is gone, an' we don't know how—an' now is your father an' me to lie down an' die in desolation widout a child to shed a tear over us, or to put up one prayer for our happiness?"

The young man's eyes filled with tears; but his cheek reddened, and he dashed them hastily aside.

"No, my boy, my glorious boy, won't refuse to save his mother's heart from breakin'; ay, and his gray-haired father's too—he won't kill us both—my boy won't,—nor send us to the grave before our time!"

"Mother," said he, "if I could I—Oh! no, no. Now, it's too late—if I didn't fight him, I'd be a perjured man. You know," he added, smiling, "there's something in a Lamh Laudher's blow, as well as in the Dead Boxer's. Isn't it said, that a Lamh Laudher needn't strike two blows, when he sends his strength with one."

He stretched out his powerful arm, as he spoke, with a degree of pride, not unbecoming his youth, spirit, and amazing strength and activity.

"Do not," he added, "either vex me, or sink my spirits. I'm sworn, an' I'll fight him. That's my mind, and it will not change."

The whole party felt, by the energy and decision with which he spoke the last words, that he was immovable. His resolution filled them with melancholy, and an absolute sense of death. They left him, therefore, in silence, with the exception of his parents, whose grief was bitter and excessive.

When the Dead Boxer heard that he had been challenged, he felt more chagrin than satisfaction, for his avarice was disappointed; but when he understood from those members of the corporation who waited on him, that Lamh Laudher was the challenger, the livid fire of mingled rage and triumph which blazed in his large bloodshot eyes absolutely frightened the worthy burghers.

"I'm glad of that," said he—"here, Joe, I desire you to go and get a coffin made, six feet long and properly wide—we will give him room enough; tehee! tehee! tehee!—ah! tehee! tehee! tehee! I'm glad, gentlemen. Herr! agh! tehee! tehee! I'm glad, I'm glad."

In this manner did he indulge in the wild and uncouth glee of a savage as ferocious as he was powerful.

"We have a quare proverb here, Misther Black," said one of the worthy burghers, "that, be my sowl, may be you never heard!"

"Tehee! tehee! agh! What is that?" said the Boxer, showing his white teeth and blubber lips in a furious grin, whilst the eyes which he fastened on the poor burgher blazed up once more, as if he was about to annihilate him.

"What is it, sar?"

"Faith," said the burgher, making towards the door, "I'll tell you that when I'm the safe side o' the room—devil a ha'porth bar-rin' that neither you nor any man ought to reckon your chickens before they are hatched. Make money of that;" and after having discharged this pleasantry at the black, the worthy burgher made a hasty exit down stairs, followed at a more dignified pace by his companions.

The Dead Boxer, in preparing for battle, observed a series of forms peculiar to himself, which were certainly of an appalling character. As a proof that the challenge was accepted, he ordered a black flag, which he carried about with him, to wave from a window of the inn, a circumstance which thrilled all who saw it with an awful certainty of Lamh Laudher's death. He then gave order for the drums to be beaten, and a dead march to be played before him, whilst he walked slowly up the town and back, conversing occasionally with some of those who immediately surrounded him. When he arrived nearly opposite the market-house, some person pointed out to him a small hut that stood in a situation isolated from the other houses of the street.

"There," added his informant, "is the house where Lamh Laudher Oge's aunt lives, and where he himself has lived since he left his father's."

"Ah!" said the black, pausing, "is he within, do you think?"

One of the crowd immediately inquired, and replied to him in affirmative.

The Dead Boxer

"Will any of you," continued the boxer, "bring me over a half-hundred weight from the market crane? I will show this fellow what a poor chance he has. If he is so strong in the arm and active as is reported, I desire he will imitate me. Let the music stop a moment."

The crowd was now on tiptoe, and all necks were stretched over the shoulders of those who stood before them, in order to see, if possible, what the feat could be which he intended to perform. Having received the half-hundred weight from the hands of the man who brought it, he approached the widow's cottage, and sent in a person to apprize *Lamh Laudher* of his intention to throw it over the house, and to request that he would witness this proof of his strength. Lamh Laudher delayed a few minutes, and the Dead Boxer stood in the now silent crowd, awaiting his appearance, when accidentally glancing into the door, he started as if stung by a serpent. A flash and a glare of his fierce blazing eyes followed.

"Ha! damnation! true as hell!" he exclaimed, "she's with him! Ha!—the Obeah woman was right—the Obeuh woman was right. Guilt, guilt, guilt! Ha!"

With terror and fury upon his huge dark features, he advanced a step or two into the cottage, and in a voice that resembled the under-growl of an enraged bull, said to his wife, for it was she—"You will never repeat this—I am aware of you; I know you now! Fury! prepare yourself; I say so to both. Ha!" Neither she nor Lamh Laudher had an opportunity of replying to him, for he ran in a mood perfectly savage to the half-hundred weight, which he caught by the ring, whirled it round him two or three times, and, to the amazement of the mob who were crowded about him, flung it over the roof of the cottage.

Lamh Laudher had just left the cabin in time to witness the feat, as well as to observe more closely the terrific being in his full strength and fury, with whom he was to wage battle on the following day. Those who watched his countenance, observed that it blanched for a moment, and that the color came and went upon his cheek.

"Now, young fellow," said the Boxer, "get behind the cabin and throw back the weight."

Lamh Landher hesitated, but was ultimately proceeding to make the attempt, when a voice from the crowd, in tones that were evidently disguised, shouted—

"Don't be a fool, young man; husband your strength, for you will want it."

The Dead Boxer started again—"Ha!" he exclaimed, after listening acutely, "fury of hell! are you there? ha! I'll grasp you yet, though."

The young man, however, felt the propriety of this friendly caution. "The person who spoke is right," said he, "whoever he is. I will husband, my strength," and he passed again into the cabin.

The boxer's countenance exhibited dark and flitting shadows of rage. That which in an European cheek would have been the redness of deep resentment, appeared, on his, as the scarlet blood struggled with the gloomy hue of his complexion, rather like a tincture that seemed to borrow its character more from the darkness of his soul, than from the color of his skin. His brow, black and lowering as a thunder-cloud, hung fearfully over his eyes, which he turned upon Lamh Laudher when entering the hut, as if he could have struck him dead with a look. Having desired the drums to beat, and the dead march to be resumed, he proceeded along the streets until he arrived at the inn, from the front of which the dismal flag of death flapped slowly and heavily in the breeze. At this moment the death-bell of the town church tolled, and the sexton of the parish bustled through the crowd to inform him that the grave which he had ordered to be made was ready.

The solemnity of these preparations, joined to the almost superhuman proof of bodily strength which he had just given, depressed every heart, when his young and generous adversary was contrasted with him. Deep sorrow for the fate of Lamh Laudher prevailed throughout the town; the old men sighed at the folly of his rash and fatal obstinacy, and the females shed tears at the sacrifice of one whom all had loved. From the inn, hundreds of the crowd rushed to the church-yard, where they surveyed the newly made grave with shudderings and wonder at the strangeness of the events which had occurred in the course of the day. The death music, the muffled drums, the black flag, the mournful tolling of the sullen bell,

The Dead Boxer

together with the deep grave that lay open before them, appeared rather to resemble the fearful pageant of a gloomy dream, than the reality of incidents that actually passed before their eyes. Those who came to see the grave departed with heaviness and a sad foreboding of what was about to happen; but fresh crowds kept pouring towards it for the remainder of the day, till the dusky shades of a summer night drove them to their own hearths, and left the churchyard silent.

The appearance of the Dead Boxer's wife in the house where Lamh Laudher resided, confirmed, in its worst sense, that which Nell M'Collum had suggested to him. It is unnecessary to describe the desolating sweep of passion which a man, who, like him, was the slave of strong resentments, must have suffered. It was not only from motives of avarice and a natural love of victory that he felt anxious to fight: to these was now added a dreadful certainty that Lamh Laudher was the man in existence who had inflicted on him an injury, for which nothing but the pleasure of crushing him to atoms with his hands, could atone. The approaching battle therefore, with his direst enemy, was looked upon by the Dead Boxer as an opportunity of glutting his revenge. When the crowd had dispersed, he called a waiter, and desired him to inquire if his wife had returned. The man retired to ascertain, and the Boxer walked backwards and forwards in a state of mind easily conceived, muttering curses and vows of vengeance against her and Lamh Laudher. After some minutes he was informed that she had not returned, upon which he gave orders that on the very instant of her appearance at the inn, she should be sent to him. The waiter's story in this instance was incorrect; but the wife's apprehension of his violence, overcame every other consideration, and she resolved for some time to avoid him. He had, in fact, on more than one occasion openly avowed his jealousy of her and O'Rorke, and that in a manner which made the unhappy woman tremble for her life. She felt, therefore, from what had just occurred at Widow Rorke's cabin, that she must separate herself from him, especially as he was susceptible neither of reason nor remonstrance. Every thing conspired to keep his bad passions in a state of tumult. Nell M'Collum, whom he wished to consult once more upon the recovery of his money, could not be found. This, too, galled him; for avarice, except during the whirlwind of jealousy, was the basis of his character—the predominant passion of his heart. After cooling a little, he called for his servant, who had been in the habit of acting for him in the capacity of second, and began, with his assistance, to make preparations for to-morrow's battle.

CHAPTER VII.

Nothing now could exceed the sympathy which was felt for young Lamh Laudher, yet except among his immediate friends, there was little exertion made to prevent him from accelerating his own fate. So true is it that public feeling scruples not to gratify its appetite for excitement, even at the risk or actual cost of human life. His parents and relations mourned him as if he had been already dead. The grief of his mother had literally broken down her voice so much, that from hoarseness, she was almost unintelligible. His aged father sat and wept like a child; and it was in vain that any of their friends attempted to console them. During the latter part of the day, every melancholy stroke of the death bell pierced their hearts; the dead march, too, and the black flag waving, as if in triumph over the lifeless body of their only son, the principal support of their declining years, filled them with a gloom and terror, which death, in its common shape, would not have inspired. This savage pageant on the part, of the Dead Boxer, besides being calculated to daunt the heart of any man who might accept his challenge, was a cruel mockery of the solemnities of death. In this instance it produced such a sensation as never had been felt in that part of the country. An uneasy feeling of wild romance, mingled with apprehension, curiosity, fear, and amazement, all conspired to work upon the imaginations of a people in whom that quality is exuberant, until the general excitement became absolutely painful.

Perhaps there was not one among his nearest friends who felt more profound regret for having been the occasion of his disgrace, and consequently of the fate to which he had exposed him, than Meehaul Neil. In the course of that day he sent his father to old Lamh Laudher, to know if young O'Rorke would grant him an interview, the object of which was to dissuade him from the battle.

"Tell him," said the latter, with a composure still tinged with a sorrowful spirit, "that I will not see him to-day. To-morrow I may, and if I don't, tell him, that for his sister's sake, he has my forgiveness."

The introduction of the daughter's name shortened the father's visit, who left him in silence.

Ellen, however, had struggles to endure which pressed upon her heart with an anguish bitter in proportion to the secrecy rendered necessary by the dread of her relations. From the moment she heard of Lamh Laudher's challenge, and saw the funeral appendages with which the Dead Boxer had darkened the preparations for the fight, she felt her heart sink, from a consciousness that she had been indirectly the murderess of her lover. Her countenance became ghastly pale, and her frame was seized with a tremor which she could hardly conceal. She would have been glad to have shed tears, but tears were denied her. Except the Boxer's wife, there was no one to whom she could disclose her misery; but alas! for once, that amiable creature was incapable of affording her consolation. She herself, felt distress resulting from both the challenge, and her husband's jealousy, almost equal to that of Ellen.

"I know not how it is," said she, "but I cannot account for the interest I feel in that young man. Yes, surely, it is natural, when we consider that I owe my life to him. Still, independently of that, I never heard his voice, that it did not fall upon my heart like the voice of a friend. We must, if possible, change his mind,", she added, wiping away her tears; "for I know that if he fights that terrible man, he will be killed."

At Ellen's request, she consented to see Lamh Laudher, with a view of entreating him, in her name, to decline the fight. Nor were her own solicitations less urgent. With tears and grief which could not be affected, she besought him not to rush upon certain death—said that Ellen could not survive it—pleaded the claims of his aged parents, and left no argument untouched that could apply to his situation and conduct. Lamh Laudher, however, was inexorable, and she relinquished an attempt that she felt to be ineffectual. The direction of her husband's attention so unexpectedly to widow Rorke's I cabin, at that moment, and his discovery of her interview with Lamh Laudher, determined her, previously acquainted as she had been with his jealousy, to keep out of his reach, until some satisfactory explanation could be given. Ellen, however, could not rest; her grief had so completely overborne all other considerations, that she cared little, now, whether her friends perceived it or not. On one thing, she was fixed, and that was, to prevent Lamh Laudher from encountering the Dead Boxer. With this purpose she wrapped herself in a cloak about ten o'clock, and careless whether she was observed or not, went directly towards his aunt's house. About two-thirds of the way had probably been traversed, when a man, wrapped up in a cloak, like herself, accosted her in a low voice, not much above a whisper.

"Miss Neil," said he, "I don't think it would be hard to guess where you are going."

"Who are you that asks?" said Ellen. "No matter; but if you happen to see young O'Rorke to-night, I have a message to send him that may serve him."

"Who are you?" again inquired Ellen. "One that cautions you to beware of the Dead Boxer; one that pities and respects his unfortunate wife; and one who, as I said, can serve O'Rorke."

"For God's sake, then, if you can, be quick; for there's little time to be lost," said Ellen.

"Give him this message," replied the man, and he whispered half a dozen words into her ear.

"Is that true?" she asked him; "and may he depend upon it?"

"He may, as there's a God above me. Good night!" He passed on at a rapid pace. When Ellen entered his aunt's humble cabin, Lamh Laudher had just risen from his knees. Devotion, or piety if you will, as it is in many cases, though undirected by knowledge, may be frequently found among the peasantry associated with objects that would appear to have little connection with it. When he saw her he exclaimed with something like disappointment:—

"Ah! Ellen dear, why did you come? I would rather you hadn't crossed me now, darling."

His manner was marked by the same melancholy sedateness which we have already described. He knew the position in which he stood, and did not attempt to disguise what he felt. His apparent depression, however, had a dreadful effect upon Ellen, who sat down on a stool, and threw back the hood of her cloak; but the aunt placed a little circular arm-chair for her somewhat nearer the fire. She declined it in a manner that argued something like incoherence, which occasioned O'Rorke to, glance at her most earnestly. He started, on observing the wild lustre of her eye, and the woebegone paleness of her cheek.

"Ellen," said he, "how is this? Has any thing frightened you? Merciful mother! aunt, look at her!"

The distracted girl sank before him on her knees, locked her hands together, and while her eyes sparkled with an unsettled light, exclaimed—

"John!—John!—Lamh Laudher Oge—forgive me, before you die! I have murdered you!"

"Ellen love, Ellen"—

"Do you forgive me? do you? Your blood is upon me, Lamh Laudher Oge!"

"Heavens above! Aunt, she's turned! Do I forgive you, my heart's own treasure? How did you ever offend me, my darling? You. know you never did. But if you ever did, my own Ellen, I do forgive you."

"But I murdered you—and that was because my brother said he would do it—an' I got afraid, John, that he might do you harm, an' afraid to tell you too—an'—an' so you promise me you won't fight the Dead Boxer? Thank God! thank God! then your blood will not be upon me!"

"Aunt, she's lost," he exclaimed; "the brain of my *colleen dhas* is turned!"

"John, won't you save me from the Dead Boxer? There's nobody able to do it but you, Lamh Laudher Oge!"

"Aunt, aunt, my girl's destroyed," said John, "her heart's broke! Ellen!"

"But to-morrow, John—to-morrow—sure yo' won't fight him to-morrow?—if you do—if you do he'll kill you—an' 'twas I that—that"——

O'Rorke had not thought of raising her from the posture in which she addressed him, so completely had he been overcome by the frantic vehemence of her manner. He now snatched her up, and placed her in the little arm-chair alluded to; but she had scarcely been seated in it, when her hands became clenched, her head sank, and the heavy burthen of her sorrows was forgotten in a long fit of insensibility.

Lamh Laudher's distraction and alarm prevented him from rendering her much assistance; but the aunt was more cool, and succeeded with considerable difficulty in restoring her to life. The tears burst in thick showers from her eyelids, she drew her breath vehemently and rapidly, and, after looking wildly around her, indulged in that natural grief which relieves the heart by tears. In a short time she became composed, and was able to talk collectedly and rationally.

This, indeed, was the severest trial that Lamh Laudher had yet sustained. With all the force of an affection as strong and tender as it was enduring and disinterested, she urged him to relinquish his determination to meet the Dead Boxer on the following day. John soothed her, chid her, and even bantered her, as a cowardly girl, unworthy of being the sister of Meehaul Neil, but to her, as well as to all others who had attempted to change his purpose, he was immovable. No; the sense of his disgrace had sunk too deep into his heart, and the random allusions just made by Ellen herself to the Dead Boxer's villainy, but the more inflamed his resentment against him.

On finding his resolution irrevocable, she communicated to him in a whisper the message which the stranger had sent him. Lamh Laudher, after having heard it, raised his arm rapidly, and his eye gleamed with something like the exultation of a man who has discovered a secret that he had been intensely anxious to learn. Ellen could now delay no longer, and their separation resembled that of persons who never expected to meet again. If Lamh Laudher could at this moment have affected even a show of cheerfulness, in spite of Ellen's depression it would have given her great relief. Still, on her part, their parting was a scene of agony and distress which no description could reach, and on his, it was sorrowful and tender; for neither felt certain that they would ever behold each other in life again.

A dark sunless morning opened the eventful day of this fearful battle. Gloom and melancholy breathed a sad spirit over the town and adjacent country. A sullen breeze was abroad, and black clouds drifted slowly along the heavy sky. The Dead Boxer again had recourse to his pageantries of death. The funeral bell tolled heavily during the whole morning, and the black flag flapped more dismally in the sluggish blast than before. At an early hour the town began to fill with myriads of people. Carriages and cars, horsemen and pedestrians, all thronged in one promiscuous stream towards the scene of interest. A dense multitude stood before the inn, looking with horror on the death flag, and watching for a glimpse of the fatal champion. From this place hundreds of them passed to the house of Lamh Laudher More, and on hearing that the son resided in his aunt's they hurried towards her cabin to gratify themselves with a sight of the man who dared to wage battle with the Dead Boxer. From this cabin, as on the day before, they went to the church-yard, where a platform had already been erected beside the grave. Against the railings of the platform stood the black coffin intended for Lamh Laudher, decorated with black ribbons that fluttered gloomily in the blast. The sight of this and of the grave completed the wonder and dread which they felt. As every fresh mass of the crowd arrived, low murmurs escaped them, they raised their heads and eyes exclaiming—

"Poor Lamh Laudher! God be merciful to him!"

As the morning advanced, O'Rorke's faction, as a proof that they were determined to consider the death of their leader as a murder, dressed themselves in red ribbons, a custom occasionally observed in Ireland even now, at the funerals of those who have been murdered. Their appearance passing to and fro among the crowd made the scene with all its associations absolutely terrible. About eleven o'clock they went in a body to widow Rorke's, for the purpose of once more attempting to dissuade him against the fight. Here most unexpected intelligence awaited them—*Lamh Laudher Oge* had disappeared. The aunt stated that he had left the house with a strange man, early that morning, and that he had not returned. Ere

The Dead Boxer

many minutes the rumor was in every part of the town, and strong disappointment was felt, and expressed against him in several round oaths, by the multitude in general. His father, however, declared his conviction that his son would not shrink from what he had undertaken, and he who had not long before banished him for cowardice, now vouched for his courage. At the old man's suggestion, his friends still adhered to their resolutions of walking to the scene of conflict in a body. At twenty minutes to twelve o'clock, the black flag was removed from the inn window, the muffled drums beat, and the music played the same dead march as on the days of uttering the challenge. In a few minutes the Dead Boxer, accompanied by some of the neighboring gentry, made his appearance, preceded by the flag. From another point, the faction of Lamb Laudher fluttering in blood-red ribbons, marched at a solemn pace towards the church-yard. On arriving opposite his aunt's, his mother wept aloud, and with one voice all the females who accompanied her, raised the Irish funeral cry. In this manner, surrounded by all the solemn emblems of death, where none was dead, they slowly advanced until they reached the platform. The Dead Boxer, attended by his own servant, as second, now ascended the stage, where he stood for a few minutes, until his repeater struck twelve. That moment he began to strip, which having done, he advanced to the middle of the stage, and in a deep voice required the authorities of the town to produce their champion. To this no answer was returned, for not a man of them could account for the disappearance of Lamh Laudher. A wavy motion, such as passes over the forest top under a low blast, stirred the whole multitude; this was the result of many feelings, but that which prevailed amongst them was disappointment. A second time the Dead Boxer repeated the words, but except the stir and hum which we have described, there was not a voice heard in reply. Lamh Laudher's very friends felt mortified, and the decaying spirit of Lamh Laudher More rallied for a moment. His voice alone was heard above the dead silence,—

"He will come, back," said he, "my son will come; and I would now rather see him dead than that he should fear to be a man."

He had scarcely spoken, when a loud cheer, which came rapidly onward, was heard outside the church-yard. A motion and a violent thrusting aside, accompanied by a second shout, "he's here!" gave intimation of his approach. In about a minute, to the manifest delight of all present, young Lamh Laudher, besmeared with blood, leaped upon the platform. He looked gratefully at the crowd, and in order to prevent perplexing inquiries, simply said—

"Don't be alarmed—I had a slight accident, but I'm not the worse of it."

The cheers of the multitude were now enough to awaken the dead beneath them; and when they had ceased, his father cried out—

"God support you, boy—you're my true son; an' I know you'll show them what the Lamh Laudher blood an' the Lamh Laudher blow is."

The young man looked about him for a moment, and appeared perplexed.

"I'm here alone," said he; "is there any among you that will second me?"

Hundreds immediately volunteered this office; but there was one who immediately sprung upon the stage, to the no small surprise of all present—it was Meehaul Neil. He approached Lamh Laudher and extended his hand, which was received with cordiality.

"Meehaul," said O'Rorke, "I thank you for this."

"Do not," replied the other; "no man has such a right to stand by you now as I have. I never knew till this mornin' why you did not strike me the last night we met."

The Dead Boxer stood with his arms folded, sometimes looking upon the crowd, and occasionally glaring at his young' and fearless antagonist. The latter immediately stripped, and when he "stood out erect and undaunted upon the stage, although his proportions were perfect, and his frame active and massy, yet when measured with the Herculean size of the Dead Boxer, he appeared to have no chance.

"Now," said he to the black, "by what rules are we to fight?"

"If you consult me," said the other, "perhaps it is best that every man should fight as he pleases. You decide that. I am the challenger."

"Take your own way, then," said O'Rorke; "but you have a secret, black—do you intend to use it?"

"Certainly, young fellow."

"I have my secret, too," said Lamh Laudher; "an' now I give you warning that I will put it in practice."

"All fair; but we are losing time," replied the man of color, putting himself in an attitude. "Come on."

Their seconds stood back, and both advanced to the middle of the stage. The countenance of the black, and his huge chest, resembled rather a colossal statue of bronze, than the bust of a human being. His eye gleamed at Lamh Laudher with baleful flashes of intense hatred. The spectators saw, however, that the dimensions of Lamh Laudher gained considerably by his approximation to the black. The dusky color of the Boxer added apparently to his size, whilst the healthful light which lay upon the figure of his opponent took away, as did his elegance, grace, and symmetry, from the uncommon breadth and fulness of his bust.

Several feints were made by the black, and many blows aimed, which Lamh Laudher, by his natural science and activity, parried; at length a blow upon the temple shot him to the boards with great violence, and the hearts of the spectators, which were all with him, became fearfully depressed.

O'Rorke, having been raised, shook his head as if to throw off the influence of the blow. Neil afterwards declared that when coming to the second round, resentment and a sense of having suffered in the opinion of the multitude by the blow which brought him down, had strung his muscular power into such a state of concentration, that his arms became as hard as oak. On meeting again he bounded at the Boxer, and by a single blow upon the eye-brow felled him like an ox. So quickly was it sent home, that the black had not activity to guard against it; on seeing which, a short and exulting cheer rose from the multitude. We are not now giving a detailed account of this battle, as if reporting it for a newspaper; it must suffice to say, that Lamh

Laudher was knocked down twice, and the Dead Boxer four times, in as many rounds. The black, on coming to the seventh round, laughed, whilst the blood trickled down his face. His frame appeared actually agitated with inward glee, and indeed a more appalling species of mirth was never witnessed.

It was just when he approached Lamh Laudher, chuckling hideously, his black visage reddened with blood, that a voice from the crowd shouted—

"He's laughing—the blow's coming—O'Rorke, remember your instructions."

The Boxer advanced, and began a series of feints, with the intention of giving that murderous blow which he was never known to miss. But before he could put his favorite stratagem in practice, the activity of O'Rorke anticipated his *ruse*, for in the dreadful energy of his resentment he not only forgot the counter-secret which had been, confided to him, but every other consideration for the moment. With the spring of a tiger he leaped towards the black, who by the act was completely thrown off his guard. This was more than O'Rorke expected. The opportunity, however, he did not suffer to pass; with the rapidity of lightning he struck the savage on the neck, immediately under the ear. The Dead Boxer fell, and from his ears, nostrils, and mouth the clear blood sprung out, streaking, in a fearful manner, his dusky neck and chest. His second ran to raise him, but his huge woolly head fell from side to side with an appearance of utter lifelessness. In a few minutes, however, he rallied, and began to snort violently, throwing his arms and limbs about him with a quivering energy, such as, in strong men who die unwasted by disease, frequently marks the struggle of death. At length he opened his eyes, and after fastening them upon his triumphant opponent with one last glare of hatred and despair, he ground his teeth, clenched his gigantic hands, and stammering out, "Fury of hell! I—I—damnation!" This was his last exclamation, for he suddenly plunged again, extended his shut fist towards Lamh Laudher, as if he would have crushed him even in death, then becoming suddenly relaxed, his head fell upon his shoulder, and after one groan, he expired on the very spot where he had brought together the apparatus of death for another.

CHAPTER VIII.

When the spectators saw and heard what had occurred, their acclamations rose to the sky; cheer after cheer pealed from the graveyard over a wide circuit of the country. With a wild luxury of triumph they seized O'Rorke, placed him on their shoulders, and bore him in triumph through every street in the town. All kinds of mad but good-humored excesses were committed. The public houses were filled with those who had witnessed the fight, songs were sung, healths were drank, and blows given. The streets, during the remainder of the day, were paraded by groups of his townsmen belonging to both factions, who on that occasion buried their mutual animosity in exultation for his victory.

The worthy burghers of the corporation, who had been both frightened and disgusted at the dark display made by the Dead Boxer previous to the tight, put his body in the coffin that had been intended for Lamh Laudher, and without any scruple, took it up, and went in procession with the black flag before them, the death bell again tolling, and the musicians playing the dead march, until they deposited his body in the inn.

After Lamh Laudher had been chaired by the people, and borne throughout every nook of the town, he begged them to permit him to go home. With a fresh volley of shouts and hurras they proceeded, still bearing him in triumph towards his father's house, where they left him, after a last and deafening round of cheers. Our readers can easily fancy the pride of his parents and friends on receiving him.

"Father," said he, "my name's' cleared. I hope I have the Lamh Laudher blood in me still. Mother, you never doubted me, but you wor forced to give way."

"My son, my son," said the father, embracing him, "my noble boy! There never was one of your name like you. You're the flower of us all!"

His mother wept with joy and pressed him repeatedly to her heart; and all his relations were as profuse as they were sincere in their congratulations.

"One thing troubles us," observed his parents, "what will become of his wife? John dear," said his mother, "my heart aches for her."

"God knows and so does mine," exclaimed the father; "there is goodness about her."

"She is freed from a tyrant and a savage," replied their son, "for he was both, and she ought to be thankful that she's rid of him. But you don't know that there was an attempt made on my life this mornin'."

On hearing this, they were all mute with astonishment.

"In the name of heaven how, John?" they inquired with one voice.

"A red-haired man came to my aunt's," he continued, "early this mornin', an' said if I wanted to hear something for my good, I would follow him. I did so, an' I observed that he eyed me closely as we went along. We took the way that turns up the Quarry, an' afther gettin' into one of the little fir groves off the road, he made a stab at my neck, as I stooped to tie my shoe that happened to be loose. As God would have it, he only tore the skin above my forehead. I pursued the villain on the spot, but he disappeared among the trees, as if the earth had swallowed him. I then went into Darby Kavanagh's, where I got my breakfast; an' as I was afraid that you might by pure force prevent me from meetin' the black, I didn't stir out of it till the proper time came."

This startling incident occasioned much discussion among his friends, who of course were ignorant alike of the person who had attempted his assassination, and of the motives which could have impelled him to such a crime. Several opinions were advanced upon the circumstance, but as it had failed, his triumph over the Dead Boxer, as unexpected as it was complete, soon superseded it, and many a health was given "to the best man that ever sprung from the blood of the Lamh Laudhers!" for so they termed him, and well had he earned the epithet. At this moment an incident occurred which considerably subdued their enjoyment. Breen, the constable, came to inform them that Nell McCollum, now weltering in her blood, and at the point of death, desired instantly to see them.

Our readers have been, no doubt, somewhat surprised at the sudden disappearance of Nell. This artful and vindictive woman had, as we have stated, been closely dogged through all her turnings and windings, by the emissaries of Mr. Brookleigh. For this haunt where she was in the habit of meeting her private friends. The preparations,

The Dead Boxer

however, for the approaching fight, and the tumult it excited in the town, afforded her an opportunity of giving her spies the slip. She went, on the evening before the battle, to a small dark cabin in one of the most densely inhabited parts of the town, where, secure in their privacy, she found Nanse M'Collum, who had never left the town since the night of the robbery, together with the man called Rody, and another hardened ruffian with red hair.

"*Dher ma chuirp*," said she, without even a word of precious salutation, "but I'll,lay my life that Lamh Laudher bates the black. In that case he'd be higher up wid the town than ever. He knocked him down last night."

"Well," said Rody, "an' what if he does? I would feel rather satisfied at that circumstance. I served the black dog for five years, and a more infernal tyrant never existed, nor a milder or more amiable woman than his wife. Now that you have his money, the sooner the devil gets himself the better."

"To the black *diouol* wid yourself an' your Englified *gosther*," returned Nell indignantly; "his wife! *Damno' orth*, don't make my blood boil by speaking a word in her favor. If Lamh Laudher comes off best, all I've struv for is knocked on the head. *Dher Chiernah*, I'll crush the sowl of his father or I'll not die happy."

"Nell, you're bittherer than soot, and blacker too," observed Rody.

"Am I?" said Nell, "an' is it from the good crathur that was ready, the other night, to murdher the mild innocent woman that he spakes so well of, that we hear sich discoorse?"

"You're mistaken there, Nelly," replied Body; "I had no intention of taking away her life, although I believe my worthy comrade here in the red hair, that I helped out of a certain gaol once upon a time, had no scruples."

"No, curse the scruple!" said the other.

"I was in the act of covering her eyes and mouth to prevent her from either knowing her old servant or making a noise, — but d — — it, I was bent to save her life that night, rather than take it," said Rody.

"I know this friend of yours, Rody, but a short time," observed Nell; "but if he hasn't more spunk in him than yourself, he's not worth his feedin'."

"Show me," said the miscreant, "what s to be done, life or purse—an' here's your sort for both."

"Come, then," said Nell, "by the night above us, we'll thry your mettle."

"Never heed her," observed Nanse; "aunt, you're too wicked an' revengeful."

"Am I?" said the aunt. "I tuck an oath many a year ago, that I'd never die till I'd put sharp sorrow into Lamh Laudher's sowl. I punished him through his daughter, I'll now grind the heart in him through his son."

"An' what do you want to be done inquired the red man.

"Come here, an' I'll tell you that," said Nell.

A short conversation took place between them, behind a little partition which divided the kitchen from two small sleeping rooms, containing a single bed each.

"Now," said Nell, addressing the whole party, "let us all be ready to-morrow, while the whole town's preparin' for the fight, to slip away as well disguised as we can, out of the place; by that time you'll have your business done, an' your trifle o' money earned;" she directed the last words to the red-haired stranger.

"You keep me out of this secret?" observed Body.

"It's not worth knowin'," said Nell; "I was only thryin' you, Rody. It's nothing bad. I'm not so cruel as you think. I wouldn't take the wide world an' shed blood wid my own hands. I tried it once on Lamh Laudher More, an' when I thought I killed him hell came into me. No; that I may go *below* if I would!"

"But you would get others to do it, if you could," said Rody.

"I need get nobody to do it for me," said the crone. "I could wither any man, woman, or child, off o' the earth, wid one charm, if I wished."

"Why don't you wither young Lamh Laudher then?" said Rody.

"If they fight to-morrow," replied Nell; "mind I say if they do—an' I now tell you they won't—but I say if they do—you'll see he'll go home in the coffin that's made for him—an' I know how that'll happen. Now at eleven we'll meet here if we can to-morrow."

The two men then slunk out, and with great caution proceeded towards different directions of the town, for Nell had recommended them to keep as much asunder as possible, least their grouping together might expose them to notice. Their place of rendezvous was only resorted to on urgent and necessary occasions.

The next morning, a little after the appointed hour, Nell, Rody, and Nanse McCollum, were sitting in deliberation upon their future plans of life, when he of the red hair entered the cabin.

"Well," said Nell starting up—"what was done? show me?"

The man produced a dagger slightly stained with blood.

"*Damno orrum!*" exclaimed the aged fury, "but you've failed—an' all's lost if he beats the black."

"I did fail," said the miscreant. "Why, woman if that powerful active fellow had got me in his hands, I'd have tasted the full length of the dagger myself. The d——l's narrow escape I had."

"The curse of heaven light on you, for a cowardly dog!" exclaimed Nell, grinding her teeth with disappointment. "You're a faint-hearted villain. Give me the dagger."

"Give me the money," said the man.

"For what? no, consumin' to the penny; you didn't earn it."

"I did," said the fellow, "or at all evints attempted it. Ay, an' I must have it before I lave this house, an' what is more, you must lug out my share of the black's prog."

"You'll get nothing of that," said Rody; "it was Nell here, not you, who took it."

"One hundred of it on the nail, this minnit," said the man, "or I bid you farewell, an' then look to yourselves."

"It's not mine," said Rody; "if Nell shares it, I have no objection."

"I'd give the villain the price of a rope first," she replied.

"Then I am off," said the fellow, "an' you'll curse your conduct."

Nell flew between him and the door, and in his struggle to get out, she grasped at the dagger, but failed in securing it. Rody advanced to separate them, as did Nanse, but the fellow by a strong effort attempted to free himself. The three were now upon him, and would have easily succeeded in preventing his escape had it not occurred to him that by one blow he might secure the whole sum. This was instantly directed at Rody, by a back thrust, for he stood behind him. By the rapid change of their positions, however, the breast of Nell M'Collum received the stab that was designed for another.

A short violent shriek followed, as she staggered back and fell.

"Staunch the blood," she exclaimed, "staunch the blood, an' there may be a chance of life yet."

The man threw the dagger down, and was in the act of rushing out, when the door opened, and a posse of constables entered the house. Nell's face became at once ghastly and horror-stricken, for she found that the blood could not be staunched, and that, in fact, eternity was about to open upon her.

"Secure him!" said Nell, pointing to her murderer, "secure him, an' send quick for Lamh Laudher More. God's hand is in what has happened! Ay, I raised the blow for him, an' God has sent it to my own heart. Send, too," she added, "for the Dead Boxer's wife, an' if you expect heaven, be quick."

On receiving Nell's message the old man, his son, wife, and one or two other friends, immediately hurried to the scene of death, where they arrived a few minutes after the Dead Boxer's wife.

Nell lay in dreadful agony; her face was now a bluish yellow, her eye-brows were bent, and her eyes getting dead and vacant.

"Oh!" she exclaimed, "Andy Hart! Andy Hart! it was the black hour you brought me from the right way. I was innocent till I met you, an' well thought of; but what was I ever since? an' what am I now?"

"You never met me," said the red-haired stranger, "till within the last fortnight."

"What do you mean, you unfortunate man?" asked Rody.

"Andy Hart was my name," said the man, "although I didn't go by it for some years."

"Andy Hart!" said Nell, raising herself with a violent jerk, and screaming, "Andy Hart! Andy Hart! stand over before me. Andy Hart! It is his father's voice. Oh God! Strip his breast there, an' see if there's a blood-mark on the left side."

"I'm beginnin' to fear something dreadful," said the criminal, trembling, and getting as pale as death; "there is—there is a blood-mark on the very spot she mentions—see here."

"I would know him to be Andy Hart's son, God rest him!" observed Lamh Laudher More, "any where over the world. Blessed mother of heaven!—down on your knees, you miserable crature, down on your knees for her pardon! You've murdhered your unfortunate mother!"

The man gave one loud and fearful yell, and dashed himself on the floor at his mother's feet, an appalling picture of remorse. The scene, indeed, was a terrible one. He rolled himself about, tore his hair, and displayed every symptom of a man in a paroxysm of madness. But among those present, with the exception of the mother and son, there was not such a picture of distress and sorrow, as the wife of the Dead Boxer. She stooped down to raise the stranger up; "Unhappy man," said she, "look up, I am your sister!"

"No," said Nell, "no—no—no. There's more of my guilt. Lamh Laudher More, I stand forrid, you and your wife. You lost a daughter long ago. Open your arms and take her back a blameless woman. She's your child that I robbed you of as one punishment; the other blow that I intended for you has been struck here. I'm dyin'."

A long cry of joy burst from the mother and daughter, as they rushed into each other's arms. Nature, always strongest in pure minds, even before this denouement, had, indeed, rekindled the mysterious flame of her own affection in their hearts. The father pressed her to his bosom, and forgot the terrors of the sound before him, whilst the son embraced her with a secret consciousness that she was, indeed, his long-lost sister.

"We couldn't account," said her parents, "for the way we loved you the day we met you before the magistrate; every word you said, Alice darling, went into our hearts wid delight, an' we could hardly ever think of your voice ever since, that the tears didn't spring to our eyes. But we never suspected, as how could we, that you were our child."

She declared that she felt the same mysterious attachment to them, and to her brother also, from the moment she heard the tones of his voice on the night the robbery was attempted.

"Nor could I," said Lamh Laudher Oge, "account for the manner I loved you."

Their attention was now directed to Nell, who again spoke.

"Nanse, give her back the money I robbed her of. There was more of my villainy, but God fought against me, an'—here—. You will find, it along with her marriage certificate, an' the gospel she had about her neck, when I kidnapped her, all in my pocket. Where's my son? Still, still, bad as I am, an' bad as he is, isn't he my child? Amn't I his mother? put his hand in mine, and let me die as a mother 'ud wish!"

Never could there be a more striking contrast witnessed than that between the groups then present; nor a more impressive exemplification of the interposition of Providence to reward the virtuous and punish the guilty even in this life.

"Lamh Laudher More," said she, "I once attempted to stab you, only for preventin' your relation from marryin' a woman that you knew Andy Hart had ruined. You disfigured my face in your anger too; that an' your preventing my marriage, an' my character bein' lost, whin it was known what he refused to marry me for, made me swear an oath of vengeance against you an' yours. I may now ax your forgiveness, for I neither dare nor will ax God's."

"You have mine—you have all our forgiveness," replied the old man; "but, Nell, ax God's, for it's His you stand most in need of—ax God's!"

Nell, however, appeared to hear him not.

"Is that your hand in mine, avick?" said she, addressing her son.

"It is—it is," said the son. "But, mother, I didn't, as I'm to stand before God, aim the blow at you, but at Rody."

"Lamh Laudher!" said she, forgetting herself, "I ax your forgive——."

Her head fell down before she could conclude the sentence, and thus closed the last moments of Nell M'Collum.

After the lapse of a short interval, in which Lamh Laudher's daughter received back her money, the certificate, and the gospel, her brother discovered that Rody was the person who had, through Ellen Neil, communicated to him the secret that assisted him in vanquishing the Dead Boxer, a piece of information which saved him from prosecution. The family now returned home, where they found Meehaul Neil awaiting their arrival, for the purpose of offering his sister's hand and dowry to our hero. This offer, we need scarcely say, was accepted with no sullen spirit. But Lamh Laudher was not so much her inferior in wealth as our readers may suppose. His affectionate sister divided her money between him and her parents, with whom she spent the remainder of her days in peace and tranquility. Our great-grandfather remembered the wedding, and from him came down to ourselves, as an authentic tradition, the fact that it was an unrivalled one, but that it would never have taken place were it not for the terrible challenge of the Dead Boxer.

Copyright © 2023 Esprios Digital Publishing. All Rights Reserved.